THE BLEEDING HEART

THE DJINN
BOOK TWO

LIZZY GAYLE

THE BLEEDING HEART

THE DJINN
BOOK TWO

LIZZY GAYLE

THE BLEEDING HEART

THE DJINN

LIZZY GAYLE

CITY OWL
PRESS

THE BLEEDING HEART
The Djinn, Book 2

CITY OWL PRESS
www.cityowlpress.com

Cover Design by MiblArt. All stock photos licensed appropriately.

Edited by Tee Tate.

For information on subsidiary rights, please contact the publisher at info@cityowlpress.com.

Print Edition ISBN: 978-1-64898-105-0

Digital Edition ISBN: 978-1-64898-104-3

Printed in the United States of America

ALSO BY LIZZY GAYLE

The Djinn:

The Binding Stone

The Bleeding Heart

The Blissful End

***

Fantasy Resorts:

Love at 20,000 Leagues

A Matter of Time

Glacial Heat

PRAISE FOR LIZZY GAYLE

"Gayle transports readers to an underwater utopia in *Love at 20,000 Leagues*... Devoted paranormal and sci-fi romance fans will enjoy the futuristic setting." – *Publisher's Weekly*

"A promising paranormal romance debut with intricate backstory, a fun cast of characters, and a trio of Djinn who'll have you rooting for their freedom to pursue true happily ever afters. *The Binding Stone* is a magical gem that will have readers wishing for the next in the series." – *Luna Joya, author of the Legacy series*

"I thoroughly enjoyed *The Binding Stone*, by Lizzy Gayle. What a fun, fast-paced, page-turner of a book! Leela and Jered are compelling main characters, and the supporting cast of friends, allies, and enemies keeps the story fresh and interesting. The flashbacks to Leela's long and difficult past perfectly compliment the main storyline. I can't wait for Book 2!" – *Lisa Edmonds, author of the Alice Worth series*

"Action-packed, steamy, and compulsively readable, *The Binding Stone* is a superb debut. The magic system of the story hooked me instantly...Add in romance, action, and unforgettable characters, and the author transports us to a place that is sure to enthrall any lover of fantasy." – *Kat Turner, author of the Coven Daughter series*

"Filled with magic and mayhem, *The Binding Stone* delivers a tale of twisted desires, lust for power, and a love strong enough to break the chains of betrayal." – *InD'tale*

To Greg Hickey, my biggest fan. I promised you the sequel, but didn't know you'd be reading it in Heaven.

PROLOGUE

LEELA

I GLANCE AT THE CLOCK ON THE MANTEL FOR THE TENTH TIME IN THE PAST hour. Just another ten minutes and Jered will be home, and we'll be able to go. I've been looking forward to this camping trip for a month. Waiting for the three-day weekend has been torturous, and I've cursed the fact that even with all my power, I cannot speed up time.

With a deep sigh, I settle back onto the couch, flipping on the TV. Though I cannot concentrate, the sound soothes me, filling the harsh emptiness of the small apartment. I have grown accustomed to the company of humans. Especially Jered.

Minutes later, hands slip confidently over my shoulders, and I smile.

"How on earth did you manage to sneak up on me, Jered?" I ask, watching the deep red of his aura wash over my chest. Only magicians like Jered have auras, and the color tells me he is as excited about our getaway as I am.

I turn over onto my knees, ready to give him a proper greeting, but the man standing behind me is not Jered. He is tall and well built with dark-auburn hair and piercing blue eyes. Handsome but cold.

"Who the hell are you?"

In answer, the magician smiles back. "It's been far too long, Leela."

Something in his voice makes me pause. I am not afraid, just uneasy. After all, there is little that can cause me harm, for I am Djinn. I study his face. He does look familiar, but I cannot place him. Power sizzles at my fingertips. I must assess whether he is a threat.

"I will ask you one more time. Who are you?"

"I'm hurt, Little One. How soon you forget the love of your life."

Cold dread pours over me. But it is impossible. I left him in a different body, sealed in a dungeon room nearly a year ago. Still, no one else but my first master, the man who betrayed and enslaved me, has ever called me that. How else would he know? I am about to demand an explanation when it hits.

Pain. Needlelike pressure all over my body. I know this pain. My eyes grow wide; I lift my hands to repel the stranger. But it isn't he who has brought the lead into my home. The pain grows stronger, and I tumble backward off the couch, striking my head on the floor.

Footsteps, then more hands beneath my arms, dragging me out toward the entryway. I strain to look around, still too shocked to panic, until I see the face of the man lifting me, setting me into a chair dragged from the small table in the corner.

But this truly is impossible. I know it. This has to be one of my nightmares that visit so often, but it feels real. And *he* is there, near seven feet tall, smooth head and beard, and rotting teeth. But if Achan is no longer in his body, then who is? Cephas is dead, killed by Taj's hands. It cannot be.

It isn't a specter wrapping heavy lead chains around my body, securing me painfully to the chair. I lick my lips, gathering enough energy to try to speak. But before I can, a woman steps out in front of me, a woman with long red hair and a cruel smile—*Kitra*. Of course. If the others are still alive, it would make sense...

"Here to kill me?" I manage to croak.

"But why would I kill someone as useful as you, Leela?"

"You have no Djinn to enslave me." I find the energy to say what I must. "No matter how you torture me, I will never put on another leash."

Kitra's laugh rings out across the small space while the other two step to either side of my chair. They are surrounding me, but still keeping a distance. The chains begin to burn through my shirt and jeans, and I shift awkwardly in the seat.

"Oh, but you see? We don't need you to put it on willingly."

"You have another Djinni?" I ask, each word costing me.

"No. We have you to thank for that, really. You see, Achan and I, we had to work together to escape our little prison. Funny that I never thought of it before. The more Djinn that work together, the more power is available to them. Well, it works the same for magicians, my pet."

My chest is too heavy to speak. My head swims. It does not surprise me that Kitra and Achan never bothered to trust another person enough to combine their powers. But I cannot point this out. I can barely stay conscious as it is.

Cephas grunts somewhere to my right. Kitra laughs.

"He hasn't been quite himself since Achan left his body," Kitra says. "He was mostly gone, but since his body survived, he was able to hang on. Unfortunately, his brain was deprived of oxygen for a little too long."

Cephas grunts again.

"Yes, Cephas. We will do it now."

Kitra reaches a hand into the air, and a long black ribbon unravels, with a gleaming diamond in the center. My eyes lock on the horrible object. My heart is attempting to escape through my chest. *This cannot be happening.*

The three people surrounding me raise their arms, and their auras pulse and swell, filling in the gaps between them with a sickly yellow light. They step forward, closing in, and the magic rolls over my body like a fog. The choker flies to my throat, wrapping itself around me, pulling tight against my pulse. It's an all too familiar feeling.

No. I am free. But the wild terror in my heart lets me know it is no longer true.

The magicians drop their arms, and the giant unravels the chains, making them disappear into thin air. The pain subsides. But the panic remains as I stay still in my seat, watching the others.

"Kneel," Kitra says.

My legs obey, and I sink to the floor before the chair.

"You will obey all three of us," Kitra says. She holds out a large, glimmering diamond, and the others step into view, each holding a matching gem. But this too is impossible—isn't it?

"So you see, if one of us were to lose our stone—even two—the third would still bind you. You had best give up any hopes of freedom now. For your own sake."

I begin to cry and shake. Tears escape and stream down my face, splashing onto the worn floorboards at Kitra's feet.

"Don't cry, Leela," Kitra says, and the tears cease, though not the tremors. "You are a very willful Djinni. You have cost us much over the years. So I cannot give you the kind of freedom you had before. From now on, you will not speak unless we ask you to or to acknowledge one of our commands. You will stay close to one of your masters at all times unless commanded otherwise. And you will address us with the proper respect. Is this understood?"

"Yes, Master." I hear the words slip from my mouth. My gaze falls at a point somewhere behind Kitra. On the backpack and sleeping bag set ready near the front door. *Jered*. It's a pain I've never known in all my years of abuse, this sudden loss of real love.

"You will take us back to our palace now," Kitra commands. "We have much work ahead of us, to rebuild an empire."

I fulfill my command, but before I do, I will one more wave of magic for Jered. A last gift to my love. I know him, know that he will not rest until he finds me. But I cannot allow this. I could not bear to watch him die. It is best if he believes I left of my own free will. He will hurt, but some other girl will mend his heart.

I clap my hands once, and the house is empty. The chair is replaced at the table, the television turned off, and the backpack and sleeping bag lay unpacked and unraveled in the small closet.

1

INTERRUPTION

TAJ

The high-pitched melody of the doorbell cuts through my head like a buzz saw. I groan and roll over, throwing the covers back over my head. *Whoever dares—*

The door sounds again, but before I can blow it to ash, my bedmate starts shaking me.

"Taj! Someone's at the door."

I don't usually pick them because of their immense brain power.

"It's five o'clock in the morning." He squeezes my bicep.

We just went to bed an hour ago. I open my eyes, and his face swims into view. Tall, lean, blond hair, and lovely gray eyes. Steven, I think.

"Taj!" Jered storms into my bedroom, thrusting the door open with a burst of magic.

I squeeze my fist tight, tempted to kill him, when I see the terror on his face. *Lee—*

"What is it, kid?" I ask, sliding out of the bed in all my glory. I know I don't look much older than him, but since in reality I'm a thousand years his senior, I have every right to call him this despite his usual protests.

His gaze darts downward for a second and then back up to my face. He appears even more upset than before.

"It's Leela. She's gone." He puts his hands on my arms, shaking me, and I repel him across the room with the flick of my finger. There are some lines you don't cross. Not even for your sister's boyfriend.

"So?" I ask, stretching.

"So? *So*? So we were supposed to be on a camping trip right now. The Grand Canyon? Remember?"

"Why do I care?" I ask, yawning. That's when I realize Steven—or is it Sam?—is clutching the covers to his chest, with his jaw hanging down. What was it he saw us do?

"You okay, sweetheart?" I ask.

This seems to snap him out of whatever state he was in, because he screams. I silence him with a wave.

"You won't remember me," I tell him, and then he disappears in a flash of green light. I sigh.

"Taj, please. Something's happened to her, I know it."

"Kid, think this through." I pick him up off the floor and get right in his face. I have to approve of Lee's taste; he is delectable. "You've been together for a year now. That's quite a bit for someone with the attention span of a Djinni. She probably got bored with you and didn't know how to tell you. That's what we do."

"No. That's what *you* do, Taj. Leela and I are in love."

"Oh, to be young and naïve."

"Taj, even if she did decide to leave me, which I know she didn't, wouldn't she have said something to you?"

I have to pause here. Lee and I have grown even closer over the past year. She is the only one I even remotely care about. Well, that's not entirely true. There is one other. The reason I stay close. The reason I'll continue to stay close no matter what Lee's done.

"How long has she been gone?" I ask, letting go and wrapping a bathrobe around myself.

Jered trails after me into the kitchen. "Sometime before I got home yesterday, around six."

"That isn't even twelve hours!" I say, throwing my hands into the air.

"She probably got distracted by some other pretty face. If you're lucky, she might even come back for you." I add the last, seeing his wounded puppy-dog look. I can be a tad harsh sometimes.

"Maybe you're right," Jered says, sinking onto a dining chair with a thoughtful frown creasing his forehead.

"Of course I am." I wave a hand, and a plate of steaming eggs and bacon appears in front of him. I hop onto the breakfast bar counter and begin working on my own morning meal. "Coffee?"

"No thanks," he says, pushing the plate away. "I just...it's a feeling, Taj. Something isn't right."

I take a sip of my conjured coffee, straight from Kona. "What could possibly have happened to her? Leela's pretty good at taking care of herself."

"Taj, she was really looking forward to this trip. She was very excited about seeing Arizona. She's never been there before." Jered leans across the counter, searching my eyes.

"Maybe she was so excited she left without you," I say through a mouthful of toast.

"I'm sorry I came." Jered pushes away from the counter. "I thought you cared about her like I do. But I guess I was wrong."

I'm in his face before his next breath, flashing my anger through my eyes, their green glow reflecting off his white shirt. "Don't you ever suggest otherwise," I hiss.

He presses closer, his face turning the color of an eggplant. "You sure act like it. You act like an uncaring asshole."

"You know, kid, you'd make a beautiful goldfish," I say, nodding toward my aquarium in the corner. His gaze follows, and he swallows.

"There must be twenty fish in there, Taj. You didn't—"

"Twenty-three," I say, releasing my grasp on his shirt. "I'd love an excuse for an even two dozen."

The moment is ruined when Jered's cell phone buzzes. He cuts it off quickly, shoving it to his ear.

"Probably her," I say, going back to my coffee.

"Slow down, Elle. What is it? Sophie?"

I slam down the cup, popping over to Jered's side.

"Okay, I'll be right over." He hangs up, and our eyes meet. "It's Sophie. She's had some kind of a nightmare, and she won't calm down. She keeps calling for me."

"Then you'd better go." Nightmares I can let him handle. But if she were in physical danger...

"Taj, Leela usually helps mask my thoughts. If Sophie listens in, she'll know."

He doesn't have to say any more. I'm the one who took the memories from her in the first place, for her own protection.

"I'll come with you," I say, exasperated. "For Sophie."

2

OOPS

Without a second thought, I flash us right outside Sophie's house. I barely get a glimpse of the impressive colonial when Jered pushes me down behind the trimmed hedge.

"What?" I snap. "I put on clothes."

"I appreciate that, Taj. I do." Jered uses his obnoxious, placating voice. "But Elle doesn't know about magic, so how can I hang up the phone and show up three seconds later?"

Oh, yeah, the mortal mother. "I only got an hour of sleep thanks to you."

Jered glares at me, fully aware sleep is a luxury I can do fine without, and peers around the corner toward the brick walkway. There's nothing there. I don't know what he's so paranoid about anyway.

"We're wasting time," I stand. "We're here now, so if Sophie's upset, I want to get in there pronto."

"Taj, we have to wait. Even if I were around the corner, I couldn't have gotten here this fast without magic."

I stroke my chin as though I'm contemplating his words. "Funny, I thought I was a free Djinni. Oh, wait, I *am* a free Djinni. So your opinion really doesn't interest me."

I snap, and we appear inside Sophie's bubblegum-colored room. Her mother is hugging her on the canopy bed while the child cries hysterically into her chest.

She's grown in just a year, into an even more beautiful little girl with honey-blond hair and crystal blue eyes. And right now, this minute, puffy red cheeks and a very runny nose.

I owe her, that tiny magician in the bed. At the tender age of eight, she managed to not only rescue me from the control of an evil master, but she granted me my freedom as well.

Jered continues to glare at me, but I ignore him and clear my throat.

The mother jumps and spins around, pulling her robe tighter across her chest. Her hair still sticks up from sleep, and she pushes at it. "Oh! Jered. Taj. How on earth did you get here so fast?"

"It wasn't that fast really," Jered says smoothly. "But we did run right over."

"I hope you don't mind my coming along, Mrs. Archer," I say with my most winning smile. "You see, Jered was at my house when you called, and it's just around the corner."

"Oh. I had no idea we lived so close." She gives up on her hair.

"Small world." I grin.

Jered's already scooted in next to Sophie, who has moved over to wrap her little arms around his waist. Her sobs quiet quickly to hiccups and sniffles. Jered conjures a handkerchief while the mother studies me. He hands it to her.

"Now, Sophie, what is it that scared you so bad?" Jered asks in the soft voice he reserves for emotional females.

She glances up at me, and it is hard not to smile. I notice the twelve-inch doll she keeps on her nightstand. Little Taj. A mini me, in a harem outfit. I couldn't resist leaving her with this last gift when I thought I'd never see her again.

"I saw the bad person take her," Sophie says in a very small voice.

"Take who?" I ask, my attention drawn back to the magicians on the bed.

"Isn't it obvious, Taj?" Jered snaps. "This is exactly what I was afraid of. It was Leela, wasn't it?" he asks.

I shoot him a keep it under control look, but it's too late. Mom is up and in hysterics before Sophie can respond.

"Leela? What happened? Jered, how could Sophie possibly know something about Leela? You're scaring her! Can't you see that? I think I better ask you to leave."

I get tired of listening somewhere around "Leela," and I wave a hand, freezing the woman in mid snit.

"Taj!" Jered yells. "Sophie."

Oops. Leela is always so much better at these situations than I am. I grin once again, but the little girl simply stares between me and her mother. Then she takes the handkerchief, wipes her nose, and flings it into the air where it disappears.

"You're one of us?" she asks.

"Human? No. I am Djinn. Here." I release the block I have on Jered's thoughts, allowing her access.

She looks toward him, stunned.

"Taj!" Jered's face flushes eggplant again. "We've been so careful—how could you?"

"Why did you make me forget?" Sophie asks, scooting away from her traitorous brother.

"I did it," I say, ignoring him and smiling at her. "I'm sorry. I was protecting you."

She glances toward the doll on her nightstand, and I nod.

"A gift," I say.

"Soph," Jered pushes, running a hand through his own sandy waves. "I need to know what you saw."

She focuses on her brother again, with that same wise, calm look I remember from whenever we were in a stressful situation. It's something I haven't mastered in a thousand years of existence, and it fills me with awe.

"It wasn't Leela," she says. Both Jered and I relax. The kid actually had me worried there for a minute. But really, who could take Lee?

"Who was it then?" Jered asks. I believe I detect a bit of disappointment in his voice. I suppose he was hoping for a lead on this conspiracy theory of his. Poor pathetic guy can't understand how Lee could have found something more interesting than him. I get it. A couple hundred years ago, I had something I thought was love, but that was naïveté. If Cal had loved me, he would have understood. Not that it would have lasted anyway since we were both slaves.

Sophie's voice pulls me out of my reverie.

"She was like them. Like Leela and Taj. Bright-green eyes that were glowing. Darker skin and curly black hair. She was very pretty, but very scared."

Jered and I exchange looks. Clearly it doesn't ring a bell for either of us. She does sound like a Djinni though. The eyes.

"What scared her?" I ask, conjuring a glass of water and offering it to Sophie.

"It was the bad one," she whispers, accepting the drink. Then she looks at me. "Can you fix my mother, please?"

"Always polite." I flick a finger at the frozen woman, and she is transferred downstairs to the kitchen with no memory of our encounter.

"Thank you," she says, pressing the cup between her palms.

"Who is this bad person?" Jered asks. "And why did you ask for me?"

"I don't know him either. I only saw him from behind. He was tall. And strong because he picked her up in one arm, after she fell. He has thick black hair like Taj."

"Another Djinni?" Jered asks, focusing his intense gaze on me.

"Let me check my psychic powers to find out," I say. Sarcasm is my best friend. "It could be," I add after a moment's consideration. "It would be almost impossible to overpower her alone otherwise."

"I saw something else," Sophie says. "That's why I asked for you, Jered."

"What did you see?" He brushes a stray hair behind her ear.

"He made a list appear in the air. He checked it after he made her fall. It had Leela's name on it. And yours, Taj."

"You saw all that?" Jered asks, voice rising in pitch to a level that makes me wince.

She nods, whimpering again. Jered stands and begins to pace. I bounce down next to Sophie, making her snivels turn to squeals, and scoop her onto my lap.

"So someone is after Djinn?" Jered asks. "That same someone could have taken Leela." The pain in his voice is clear.

"Let's not jump to conclusions," I say. "Besides, I'm not convinced this was a true vision."

"What do you mean?" Jered turns a lovely shade of pink. "You saw how upset she was. You remember her dream last year, don't you? She saw Leela saving her in Kitra's palace."

"I don't have dementia," I snap. "I remember. But realistically, who could possibly know how to find Djinn? Let alone who we are. Even I don't know all the Djinn out there. Free or enslaved."

"I don't know," Jered says, clutching his forehead. He's exhausted. It occurs to me that he may not have had much sleep either last night, and *he* actually needs it. Plus, Leela told me how when he gets stressed, he still has headaches. I guess sharing a body with a madman is bound to leave some aftereffects.

"Can you tell us exactly what you saw?" I ask Sophie. "It would help us find the missing Djinni. And maybe even Leela."

"So you do think she's in trouble?" Jered asks, placing a hand on my shoulder.

"I'm reserving judgment," I say, tolerating his touch. "How about it, Sophie?"

She rubs one lacy pink arm across her nose and looks up at me. "I don't know how. I wish I could show you."

"Maybe you can." I pull a sketch pad from the air and hand it to her. "And here's a pencil."

"I can't draw that good," she says, head falling forward.

I tip her chin upward so she can see me. "It's a magic pencil. It will help you, if you use your own magic to guide it."

Her eyes light up with possibility, and she takes the gifts in her lap. For a few minutes, all we hear is scratching as the pencil flies across the paper. Jered taps an impatient rhythm with his foot against the wall as we wait. I am about to tie him down to the bed from irritation when Sophie holds up her masterpiece.

"Oh," I say as I stare at the image on the page. "Oh. I do know her. That's Adia."

3

AUGUST 3, 1866

I FOLLOW MY NEW MASTER THROUGH THE DOORS OF THE MAIN HOUSE, *resplendent with Grecian columns and thick ivy vines that cling to the walls. She is Margaret Wilde, the widowed owner of a grand Southern plantation. In fact, the enormous white building is in such excellent repair compared to the rest of those in the surrounding areas, it is hard to believe no one is suspicious of magic. Most people were hit hard after the war, their own land used as a battle-ground or burned, and forced to free their slaves. I did what I could to help the North whenever I was able. But there's no need to tell my mistress this. I'm sure this information would not impress her.*

"A word, Charlotte," my master calls into a large sitting room to the right of the entrance.

A girl of around eighteen straightens as her name is called. She is dressed in a ruffled gown of white and holds court amid a crowd of friends and admirers, yet all attention turns to me. Mouths drop open all around. I am striking after all, having picked a body with the perfect proportion of muscle and a height of over six feet. Not to mention the picture of Southern gentility in my fine gray suit and walking cane. Well, impressive, I suppose, save the color of my skin, which I suspect is the true cause of their nervousness.

Charlotte shows no sign of anxiety, though. Despite her angelic appearance, perfect heart-shaped face, and long blond curls, I see something sharp in her gray eyes, something that reminds me of her mother. Her aura is brilliant, shiny waterfalls of blues and greens that cascade over her in a steady rhythm. No wonder she is the center of attention.

She whisks her way toward us with such a calculated sway that all eyes are drawn away from me and back to her. Impressive. I continue to stand casually behind her mother, with a practiced debonair grin on my face. Though the moment she reaches us, I swipe my hat off my head in a grand gesture, and several of her girlfriends titter. She smiles.

"Mother?"

"I will have Humphrey serve your friends some lemonade. In the meantime, I'd like you to join us in the den please."

Charlotte bids adieu to her admirers and sweeps along the corridor beside me. There's barely room with her dress taking up the majority of the hall. Gilded mirrors hang on the walls along with larger-than-life portraits of Wilde ancestry. Too hard to tell if they were magicians. Auras do not come through in paintings.

Once the door is closed behind us, the Widow Wilde's Djinni, Caldor, appears in the room. He is the one who helped secure my stone for his master. Like most of our kind, he has dark hair and skin with emerald-green eyes. His face has a pleasing roundness to it as well. Charlotte doesn't even bother a glance in his direction.

"What is this?" she asks. "I was busy, Mother."

"This is your birthday gift."

Nice.

Charlotte wrinkles her nose up and circles me. I stand perfectly still, meeting Caldor's eyes. He gives no clue as to what I'm in for. Though I have a pretty good idea. Nearly eight centuries of indentured servitude do not lie.

"Why on earth did you show him off to my friends?" Charlotte's voice rings across the room. She stamps her foot on the polished wood and pouts.

"If Taj is here to protect you, no one will ever challenge you, Lottie." It is the first time her mother has sounded soft.

"I do not need protection. If anyone bothers me, I shall turn them into caterpillars." Her fingers spark.

I raise an eyebrow but remain still, cane and hat clutched behind my back. The Widow Wilde offers a wan smile to her daughter and places *my stone in her palm. Charlotte tucks it inside her bosom and glares at me.*

"You will not interact with my friends unless I've given the command. Understood?"

I bow again.

"Hmph. And you can cut the act. I know how you really feel about this."

The grin falls from my face, and I straighten to my full height. A good foot taller than her. If it weren't for the ocean of petticoats, she'd be rather slight, actually. Not that it matters. She's taller than my last master, and he was none too fun.

"Taj, you say?" she asks.

"That is my name." It is the first I've spoken to her.

"I believe I'll call you William. A far more suitable name in case anyone should hear. You're Cal's cousin visiting from abroad. Spain, I should think. Anyone can see you have the same eyes. Now you will escort me to my rooms to familiarize yourself with this place." She spins to face her mother, nose stuck in the air. "Mother."

With that she huffs off, throwing aside the double doors and exploding into the hall, with me falling in her wake.

4

MAGIC TRACKER

"Adia?" Jered asks.

"Very good, you can repeat names." I clap my hands in mock adoration.

Sophie laughs.

"Who is she, Taj?" Jered presses. "And what does this have to do with Leela?"

"Settle down. I don't know what this has to do with Leela. Or me, for that matter. But Adia is a Djinni that passed through the veil in Africa—one of the original few. She traveled, and I crossed paths with her in Asia initially."

"Initially?" Jered asks.

"Perhaps I should just be done with it and turn you into a parrot." I stand, stretching and wishing I were still in bed with Simon.

"Sorry, but I'm worried about Leela. God knows what's already happened to her. Taj, you know what those people can do."

"People like you?" I ask, raising an eyebrow.

"You know I would never—"

"Don't get your panties in a twist. I know you wouldn't." I wave him off. "If I thought you would, you'd be dead. You freed Leela, even though you wanted her. That must have been hard."

"Not at all. Generally when you love someone, you don't want them to be enslaved. FYI, Taj."

Now it is my turn to glare. He's cupping his head in his hands again, pressing his fingers to his temples and squinting in pain. I suppose I ought to lay off. It's just so easy to torment him.

"Adia," I concede, grinning with the memory, "turned up again one other time. When I first came to America. Around the time of the American Revolution. She belonged to a man named Franklin."

"Ben Franklin?" Jered asks, dropping his hands. "You're shi—pulling my leg," he finishes, seeing Sophie watching with wide eyes.

"Scout's honor," I say, raising the obligatory three fingers. Or is it four? I don't know; I've never been a scout. "How else do you imagine he got so famous? Or had so many women? Have you seen his picture?"

"And next you're going to tell me you belonged to George Washington? That *he* was a magician?" Jered crosses his arms in challenge.

"No. My master was a man named Arnold. That didn't end well. Too bad, though. Another magician got a hold of my stone, and well, I ended up back in France for a short time. But that's a wholly different story."

"He doesn't believe you," Sophie says, tugging on my sleeve.

"Small mind," I say, scooping her up and tossing her into the air, eliciting delighted squeals.

"So back to Adia," Jered says, waving me on. "You crossed paths with her twice. Can you think of any reason someone might be after her?"

I pause, remembering. "She wasn't exactly Miss Congeniality," I muse aloud, setting Sophie down on the carpet.

"Yeah, that surprises me."

"No. She makes me look like a freaking puppy dog. So yeah, I'd believe she could have pissed someone off. But it isn't like Djinn to go after other Djinn. Unless..."

"Unless?" Jered says excitedly.

"Unless he isn't trying to hurt her at all. Maybe he's trying to rescue the others. Free them. Maybe he's been freed, and he's spreading the love." The thought is a welcome one. It might be nice to fight back for a change.

"Then what happened to Leela?" Jered asks, sinking onto the foot of the bed. He looks so forlorn, I have to put a hand on his shoulder.

"Maybe he came for her, and she thought he was hot."

He shrugs off my hand.

"Maybe I can help you find Leela," Sophie says, once again tugging on my sleeve.

"I don't think that's possible, Soph," Jered says, trying to smile but ending up looking like he's passing gas.

"Why not?" I raise an eyebrow. "She's done some pretty impossible things for a kid, and that was a year ago. Give the girl a shot."

Jered purses his lips, considering Sophie. "Okay, I guess. What's the harm in trying?"

Sophie throws her arms around her brother's neck.

"How do we do this?" Jered asks, picking her up and balancing her on his hip.

"We go to the scene of the supposed crime," I say with a wink.

And we are all sitting in the middle of Jered's apartment.

"Taj! We can't just take Sophie without her mom's permission. Look at her, she's still in her pajamas."

I take in Sophie's pink striped pajamas and knotted hair. Huh. I snap my fingers, and she's dressed in a frilly dress with two neat pigtails. "Her mother and family now believe she slept over here last night."

Jered rolls his eyes. Sophie spins in circles, making the skirt of her dress fly out like a bell. When she stops, she falls down, dizzy with giggles.

"Now what?" Jered asks.

"Let me see," Sophie says.

We watch as she closes her eyes, taking a deep breath, arms outstretched. I don't believe Jered can see what I can, her rainbow aura, stretching outward as if it's scenting the air. She walks confidently between the couch and the television, not bumping into a single thing.

Jered waits, arms folded. Doubting Thomas. I watch.

"There was someone else here recently," she says.

I perk up.

"I think they used magic because the air tingles. Right here." She points to a spot near the sofa and then continues moving around until she gets to the entryway. She stops in the center of the barren floor and gasps.

"What is it?" we both ask at the same time.

"A *lot* of tingling," she answers. "From all around."

"Have any magical guests lately?" I ask Jered.

"None that I'm aware of." His face pales, a tinge of pea green coloring his aura.

"Could it have been Lee's magic?" I ask.

"I don't think so," Sophie says, narrowing her eyes in concentration. "Some of it was, or at least it feels the same as yours does. But most of it feels like something...different."

"Different how?" Jered's practically hovering over his sister, so I step between them.

"I can't explain," Sophie says, her little shoulders slumping. "But I don't like how it feels."

"How's this supposed to help?" Jered whines, now focused on me.

"Oh, it was very helpful," I say, setting my hands on his arms. "Because now *I* believe that something happened. Something that wasn't part of Lee's plans."

5

VISITOR

"I WANT TO GO WITH YOU," JERED SAYS, AFTER WE DROP SOPHIE OFF. WE'RE sitting in his car because he insisted on bringing her home this way. I don't like cars. Unless they're parked in a secluded spot with a hot guy.

"No can do. You'd slow me down."

"I have to do something, Taj. I can't stand it. I just keep seeing her, in that cell, with that freak—"

"That 'freak' is dead. I killed him," I say, patting his knee.

He looks at my hand and slumps his shoulders.

"But he isn't the only one who's like that, is he?" He sounds like a little boy. Well, I suppose he still is. Nearly twenty-two is nothing these days.

"I'll find her." I sound confident. Good for me.

"How?"

"Djinn magic is too complicated to explain to a mere human."

"So you have no idea, do you?" He grimaces like he's been kicked in the groin.

"I'm going to talk to a few...people," I say, staring out the passenger side window.

"I just feel so useless," he says. That's too big of an opening for me. I won't take the bait. He's too upset.

"You can do something," I offer instead.

"What?" He eyes me suspiciously.

"Move your reservation to next weekend. We should have it all figured out by then." I wink.

"Taj," he says, rubbing the back of his neck. "Thank you. In all seriousness, I'd be lost without your help."

My face heats up. "You're welcome."

I pop out of the car as he pulls in his driveway. I have a friend to call on. I don't like passing back and forth between the veils of our two worlds. It is uncomfortable to do and awkward to get used to the weightless, bodiless feeling of the other side. I enjoy the physical senses far too much to truly consider staying away. But I know that for many, the dangers of the human world far outweigh any other consideration.

My body is gone, dispersed into molecules that belong in the physical realm. What remains is my essence; if it were possible to be viewed by human eyes, it would look something like a mosaic of colored wisps, constantly swirling and coalescing into a brilliant cloud of shattered rainbows. I let this self, my energy, flow through the layers of the others. I reach outward into space, feeling my way forward, toward something familiar. I brush between two others and pick up on a snippet of conversation.

...too dangerous out there.

...their own business.

Well, now my curiosity is piqued.

Before I can enfold myself around the others' energy, Mira finds me, and I remember my purpose in being here.

So you've come back.

It feels so right to connect with her energy. I hadn't realized how much I missed her presence until now. *No, Mira. I just needed to speak to you.*

Please don't tell me this is about Leela.

'Fraid so. I feel her energy shift, but I move along with her. *Wait! Mir, she's gone.*

She stops. *So? She's probably enjoying the pleasures of the flesh.*

That's almost the same thing Lee said about Rhada. And look how that turned out. I know I probably shouldn't bring it up, since remembering that particular moment might hinder more than help. But I feel her relax ever so slightly and know I've done the right thing.

What do you want from me? She—you both should have returned with me. It is less complete here without you, Taj.

I miss you too, Mir. I let my energy flow over and through her like a caress. She sighs. Or at least the equivalent of a sigh from a formless blob of energy. *Come back with me. I need to combine powers to accomplish the locator spell.*

Find another Djinni. I already did my part. We're even, remember?

And if it were me?

Ah, but it isn't.

She would do it for you.

No good. I can feel it. Mira's not budging. Not that I blame her really after what happened to us. But I had to try.

It's time to get back to the world I've come to call home. I will have to find another way. So I leave her there, pushing outward toward the barrier, and once again bump into one of the same energies I encountered on my way in.

Crossing over? it asks.

Going home, I say.

It is dangerous out there. Humans cannot be trusted.

Bigot.

The other Djinni does not answer. Probably doesn't know the concept. I push my way through and spill into my usual body, breathing in the scent of burning leaves and fresh fall air.

I spin around, meaning to go back to my apartment, when I nearly bump into someone. Apparently the other Djinni also came through. He's tall with thick dark waves of hair and the usual bright-green eyes, slender in stature, yet clearly well built—like a swimmer. Interesting choice.

"Following me?" I ask, power flowing through me at the ready.

"Thought it might be intriguing to continue our discussion." He flashes me a supermodel grin. Straight white teeth that gleam against his tanned skin. Definitely a nice drink of water.

"I'm a little busy," I say, not making a move to go.

"Too bad," he says, furrowing his brow. "I was curious about this word. Bigot."

"Don't suppose you've been sneaking around with a list of Djinn, kidnapping people?" I ask in my most flirtatious voice.

"Kidnapping people?" he asks, expression blank. A gust of wind blows the hair back from his forehead, and he blinks.

"Taking Djinn against their will? Or perhaps freeing them?" I press, sliding a fingertip along his bare arm. Wouldn't life be easy for a change if I could solve this one mystery so quickly?

He watches the goose bumps rise along his flesh where my finger touches like he's never seen such a thing before. "I'm afraid this is the first time I've visited the other side."

"Really?" I let my hand fall to my side and cock my head.

"Yes. And I must say it is quite exhilarating. This body is so...so sensual." He squeezes his own arms like he's hugging himself.

"Oh, it gets much better." I move farther into his personal space until I'm nearly pressed against him. I raise my hands, let them travel over his shoulders and down his skin. Feel him tremble beneath my touch. He opens his mouth slightly, and his breathing speeds up. I imagine the bulge starting inside his pants, and my own cock rises to the occasion.

"That is—quite nice," he says in a breathy way.

I lean in and brush my lips gently against his. He makes a little sound that I find quite attractive, and I press forward, running my hands through his hair and my tongue along his teeth. He returns my embrace, and I transport us to my apartment.

Of course, being otherwise preoccupied, I do not notice the other person in the room. Nor does she bother to move. In fact, if I hadn't broken away to look around for the bed, I wouldn't have seen her at all.

"Mira."

I let the newcomer go, and he falls unceremoniously to the carpet, panting.

Mira continues her cold stare. "Yes, Taj. Quite the emergency, I see."

"It is," I protest.

"Yet you had enough time for a tryst with Brolach?"

"Brolach?" I consider my new friend still on the floor.

"You don't even know his name?" She snorts. "Why does that not surprise me?"

"I would have gotten there eventually," I say, helping Brolach to his feet.

"I thought you were opposed to crossing over?" Mira's ire changes focus to my companion as she flips one long strand of glossy black hair behind her shoulder. She's wearing it loose, I notice, probably because Kitra made her wear it tied in a ponytail all those years. It makes me think of Lee and how she cut her own hair short after she was freed.

"I wanted to see what all the fuss was about," Brolach says. "I also wanted to ask Taj something." He colors slightly and looks away.

"And did you like his answer?" she asks, folding her arms across her chest.

"Very much." He grins, and I feel myself responding again. All over.

"Well, Taj, since you now have another Djinni to help you—" Mira raises a hand in preparation to leave, but I grab her wrist.

"Please, Mir. Don't go. You can help me because you know who we are searching for."

Her shoulders fall, and she lowers her hands with a nod.

"Why did you decide to come back?" I ask, keeping hold of her.

"I've heard rumors," she says, biting her bottom lip. It's a habit I recognize. She's worried.

"Oh?" I press, stepping into her personal space.

"Rumors of Djinn disappearing. I guess I was concerned—"

"That Leela would disappear too? You do care."

"Let's just get this over with." Mira bumps me with her shoulder as she moves toward the door.

"Brolach, I'm sorry, but I'm going to have to take my leave. I did tell you I'm busy, no?" I give an apologetic and hopefully attractive shrug.

"Perhaps I can see you again?" he asks, stepping nose to nose with me and taking my hands in his.

"I'd like that," I say.

"He can help," Mira suggests while leaning on the doorframe. "Three Djinn, we'll find her no problem."

She's brilliant. I glance at Brolach, who is still holding my hands. "If you'd be willing?"

"Certainly." He perks up. "Who are we looking for?"

"My sister, Leela."

"Sister?" Brolach questions. Mira raises her eyebrows.

"We decided that is the closest description of our relationship. What humans call siblings. Now we're going to need something she cares about for this spell." I snap my fingers, and Jered appears before me, stumbling.

"Is that—?" Brolach asks, poking a finger at Jered's bright-green aura.

"He is a magician," Mira confirms.

"Then we should kill him," Brolach says, raising a hand.

I throw my shield out in front of Jered, causing the force of Brolach's spell to knock him backward onto the bed. Smoke issues from his clothing. Which, for the first time, I realize is identical to my own. Tight black T-shirt and dark-blue jeans. No wonder I found him attractive.

"No killing this one, dearest. He belongs to my sister."

Brolach stands, rubbing his sleeves and looking confused. "But I thought it was the other way around—"

"See? You have much to learn. Lesson number one: not every human is evil."

He looks dubious but does not move to strike.

"Taj? Mira?" Jered finds his voice. "Who...?"

"Jered, Brolach. Brolach, Jered." I position Jered in the middle of us and pat his shoulders. "All right then, Jered. We're going to find Lee now. Do me a favor and stand very, very still."

6

AUGUST 3, 1866

THE MOMENT WE ENTER HER ROOMS, A TINY MAID SCUTTLES OUTSIDE LIKE SHE'S *afraid of being struck. I don't doubt that's exactly the case. Charlotte Wilde throws the doors closed and turns on me, walking forward with such purpose, I find myself backing up until I hit the window seat.*

"William, I have a very important job for you. You will make yourself useful by teaching me to be an expert lover. I'll need to know all manner of tricks in order to properly manipulate whichever man I choose."

"Pardon?" is all I can think to say. It was certainly not what I'd expected.

She slaps me hard across the face, and my head springs back the second she's done as though nothing's happened, causing her to scream in frustration.

"You will teach me how to make love in the way a man wants most! You may start by kissing me."

It takes me only moments to make up my mind as to how to follow such a command, despite my own sordid past. My third master had gaggles of children and one in particular that used to bite. The day the little sprout bit his father, my master bit him back, explaining that was the easiest and fastest way to teach the child what not to do.

Hopefully he was right.

I grab the young Miss Wilde roughly by the shoulders and press my mouth to hers while curling a hand through her hair. The myriad of pins holding it in place disappear, allowing it to cascade over her shoulders.

To my utter dismay, she seems to like it. Her breath speeds up, but I don't give her the chance to speak. Just keep moving my mouth with hers as I back her into the bed. I haven't given up yet. I still hold out hope that she does not truly mean what she says. I trail my hand over her body, and her ridiculous costume vanishes. I wedge my knee between her legs and begin roughly manhandling her as I have seen old masters do many times.

That does it. Her manner switches instantly from curiosity to panic. She struggles, scratching at my jacket, trying to call out beneath my kiss and order me to stop. I feel her heart pound against me as her gray eyes stretch with fear. It takes all I have not to laugh due to the absurdity of it all. It's probably less enjoyable to me, to be honest, but I must keep at it a moment or two more to be certain she gets the message.

I gather her hands in mine and pin them behind her head. Salty tears trickle down to my mouth, and she jerks with sobs. That is when I let her go, feeling more than a bit ill about what I've done. But if it saves her from a man all too willing, and me another lifetime of sexual abuse, this one "bite" will have been worth it.

Charlotte scrambles back up onto the bed, pulling at the blankets in an attempt to cover herself. She does have a beautiful body. Too bad it does nothing for me, or I may have been excited about her first command. I right myself, fastening my pants and tugging my jacket back into place, and then fold my arms across my chest.

"Do you not wish me to continue to fulfill your command, Master Lottie?"

"You pig!" she shouts. "You, you, you, you..."

"I've been around a long time," I say softly, sitting on the edge of the bed and ignoring her attempt to scoot farther away. "You would do well to be a bit more careful with both your words and your actions."

"How dare you?" she breathes. Her face is a lovely shade of mauve. It goes well with her corn-silk hair.

"You may beat me if you wish," I say, hoping I've gauged her right. "It is within your right. But another Djinni may not have been quite so sparing with you after such a command."

She sits motionless, save the rise and fall of her chest beneath the blanket. I *am patient. We have eternity, after all. Finally, she licks her lips and lets her shoulders fall.*

"Surely that is not the way men prefer."

"All men are different. But I know of far too many that don't care about their partner's pleasure."

Her color deepens as she draws a steadying breath. "Perhaps I am a bit... impulsive on occasion."

"There now. That wasn't so bad, was it?" I ask, standing. "I can hardly blame you, after all. I've broken many hearts in my day."

She allows a small giggle to escape her lips and then clamps them shut. I snap, and she's fully dressed once again. Hair pinned perfectly in place. My tiger's eye stone is set inside a silver brooch around her neck.

"Lovely," I say. "I'll be happy to fulfill your command verbally, over time."

"Thank you," she says, averting her gaze. "But that won't be necessary."

In answer, I offer a smile and an arm. She takes hold, and I escort her downstairs to her group of giggling girls and handsome suitors. I stand back, ready to take her cue.

"Everyone," she says sweetly, and the room falls quiet. "I'd like y'all to meet someone. This is Taj." She nods almost imperceptibly in my direction at the mention of my actual name. "He's my mother's friend's cousin, visitin' us from Spain. Isn't that nice? I'd appreciate it if everyone would give him a warm welcome. We don't want anyone thinkin' Southerners have no manners, after all."

7

UNINVITED

"Hold still. This won't hurt a bit." I'm sensing Jered may be a little nervous. Maybe it's the way he keeps swallowing and glancing over at Brolach. I need to have a talk with *that* boy about manners.

"Let's just get on with it," Jered says.

Mira, Brolach, and I link hands around him, and I concentrate on Lee's face—will myself to find her. Connect with her. My power entwines with the others, and I even feel a tug from Jered's magician's aura. How cute.

As I see the space opening up around me, feel myself flowing along with the energy trail that belongs to only her, I am torn from the hands of the others and thrown against the wall of my apartment with such force the breath is knocked from my chest. Searing pain circles my wrists and ankles as lead shackles lock me in place.

My gaze flies around the room, searching for the source of the attack. It doesn't take long to find her. Lee stands before the bedroom window, arms still outstretched toward me.

Something about her is not right. I mean besides the obvious—the choker. It's the intense, unblinking gaze, directed only at me, that is pasted on her impassive face that makes me shudder. As long as I've known her, if there's one thing Leela is, it's totally emo.

"Lee." It costs me to speak, but I have to get the attention of the others. "We were just looking for you."

"Leela!"

Jered's cry pulls her attention for a moment, and her mask breaks right along with her heart. I believe she might be in more pain than I am in this moment.

Brolach screams upon seeing me, and Mira sweeps a hand through the air toward Lee.

"No!" Jered shouts, throwing his aura out to block the attack. It isn't nearly strong enough, but it does give Lee enough time to react. With one longing glance toward Jered, she disappears from view. The blinds clatter and shake as Mira's spell hits.

"You idiot! I could have stopped her. What the hell is wrong with you?" Mira is in Jered's face, making him wince.

"I'm sorry," he says. "I thought you were going to hurt her. I had to protect her."

"Of course I was going to hurt her. But it wouldn't have killed her. And we would have had her."

"Um, excuse me," I say. "Little help?"

Brolach is the one to snap his fingers, releasing me. He offers me a hand up from the spot where I fell, and I accept, standing and massaging my rapidly healing wrists. One glance tells me Jered is dangerously close to a breakdown. He's rubbing his temples again, squinting his eyes shut, and shaking his head slowly. Mira still glares at him, arms folded. I can almost see the steam coming from her ears.

I put a hand on Jered's shoulder and squeeze. "That was good."

"Good?" he chokes out, shrugging off my hand. "I blew it!"

"Not necessarily. We've now got quite a bit more information than we started with." I stay as even and patient as possible.

"We do?" He peers up at me from beneath his wrist.

"Think about it, kid. What did you see?"

"Leela. And...and she was wearing one of those things."

"Right. So we know it was a magician. What else?"

"Her outfit. She was dressed in a red harem outfit. Like in the genie stories." Jered's eyes glass over, but he fights at the tears. I imagine he's thinking about the overt sexuality exhibited by the costume.

"That was a uniform," Mira says. Her voice is no longer angry, but cold, and she hugs herself, looking out the window.

"We know who has her," I say gently, for both their sakes.

"What? Who?"

"Those are the clothes Kitra made us wear in the beginning," Mira says, still staring outside.

"Kitra? But...no. She's dead. She's trapped. She can't. How?" Jered sits heavily on the bed.

"I don't know," I say. "But if she's alive, that would explain it. And that's why she came for me. Lee knows where I live. If I hadn't had visitors, I'd already be the newest trophy in her collection." I mash my fist into my thigh.

Mira backs up suddenly, shaking her head, eyes wide. "I have to go, Taj. I can't do this. I thought I could, but I can't. Not if it's her. I won't go back."

"Relax, Mir. As long as we stick together, there's nothing they can do. It's one against two."

"There was something else too," Jered says, standing.

"What?" I ask, trying not to take my eyes off Mira.

"Did you see her face when she first came in? And why didn't she say anything? Last time, she did her best to give us clues and information even when she was under Kitra's control."

I speak as evenly as possible. It feels like I'm near several land mines, all primed to explode at the slightest touch. "It was probably her commands. If it is Kitra, she's going to be overly cautious this time. She won't make the same mistake twice."

"We have to get her back." Jered paces between us.

"I'm sorry. I really am. But I just can't." Mira disappears in a puff of smoke before I can reach her, so I turn to Brolach.

"How about you, sweetheart? Up for a little search and rescue?"

"I don't know," he says, looking pale. "I've heard about magicians. I shouldn't have come. I was curious. But I'm not very good with the concept of pain...or bondage."

"Don't knock it till you try it." I wink in an attempt to win him over.

"Taj, we have to go." Jered grasps my shoulders. This time, I don't send him flying. "We can't endanger anyone else. We can't let Gabe happen all over again." At least he sounds much more together now.

"Gabe?" Brolach asks.

"My friend. He died last year. The same magician killed him." Jered's hands fist and fall to his sides.

"Oh dear." Brolach feels for the mattress before sitting down.

"And you aren't worried about me?" I ask, narrowing my eyes at Jered.

"I pity the poor magician who thinks she can enslave you again," Jered says with a smirk.

"You got that right, kid. But if I take you with me, I need to know up front that if the opportunity arises, you will not hesitate to kill."

Jered swallows. "I will do whatever it takes to get her back, Taj. I swear."

"Now that's what I'm talking about, Romeo."

8

HEART WRENCHING

Much to my dismay, Brolach has taken his leave. I suppose I might have come on a bit too strong, asking him to face down Kitra with us. It couldn't have been my make-out skills.

"We should have a plan before we go in," Jered says. I'm surprised the floor isn't on fire, he's been pacing back and forth so much.

I sit on the bed watching him, starting to get dizzy. "She'll be expecting us, now that Lee's gone back empty-handed."

"Taj..." Jered swallows. "If Kitra's still alive—"

"Achan could be too," I finish. "I know."

Dark swirls flow through Jered's aura, and he finally stops near the window, looking out. Though I don't think he's really enjoying the view of the lake.

I am about to tell him not to worry, that even if Achan is alive, he's probably nowhere near Kitra, when sudden piercing pain slices through my chest, and I crash to the floor. I'm vaguely aware of my arms and legs thrashing around. Of Jered running toward me. But all I can really focus on is the sensation of invisible hands attempting to rip my heart from my body.

As I am about to lose consciousness, the feeling lifts, and I am left panting on the floor. Jered's face swims into view above me. He keeps glancing around, as though searching for some hidden assailant, and then rests his eyes on me, full of concern.

I'm touched.

"I didn't see it," he says, as I accept a hand and pull myself to a sitting position.

My pulse still throbs in my ears. "Didn't see what?"

"No lead. No magicians. No Djinn," he reports.

"That wasn't from lead poisoning," I say, still gripping my stomach as I stand, leaning on the mattress.

"What? But I thought that was the only thing that could hurt you."

"I've felt this before. But it's been over a thousand years." He waits for me to continue, but I can't. I can't tell him that it means a Djinni has been killed. I have to find Mir. Have to talk to her. "I need to go."

"What? You can't go. We need to get Leela!" Jered shouts.

I throw out a hand, and he is pushed into the wall, his feet dangling inches above the ground.

"Sorry," I say. "I'll be back. I promise. Don't do anything without me. In fact, I'm going to make sure you don't." I let my hand drop, but Jered stays stuck to the wall, clearly struggling, but unable to get down.

"Taj!" he screams.

"I know you, Jered. You'll do something stupid, like try to rescue her yourself. And I can't let you get yourself killed. Lee will never forgive me." I only hope she's still alive to get mad at me in the first place.

I disappear to the tune of Jered's screams and push my way through the veil to the other world. Chaos. I should have expected it. Agony. Moans. Sobbing. Everyone and everywhere I touch is filled with misery, shock, and confusion. I ignore it as best I can and extend my essence farther, stretching out with searching fingers of energy until I find her.

Mir. It is all I can bring myself to say, despite my mad dash to get to her.

Taj? Why are you here? It wasn't—it couldn't be her.

Is that desperation I hear? *Kitra is the only one who's ever managed this.*

Silence.

Why am I here? I ask it, but I already know the answer. I cannot lose Lee. I need Mir. And I am terrified of facing Jered.

Of course Mira misunderstands me. *Please Taj, don't be angry with me.*

I do not blame you, Mir. I know how much I asked. But Lee...

We have to go see for ourselves.

Without waiting for my response, Mira pushes back through to the other realm. I follow, nearly crashing into her as I land on my bedroom floor. The first thing I notice is the lack of Jered's screams. I suppose his voice got tired.

"Where's the human?" Mira asks.

"What?"

"I just assumed he'd still be here, wanting to find Lee. Or did he jump out the window when he found out?"

I can't answer her because I'm too busy scraping my chin off the floor.

"Taj? We should go—"

"That's impossible," I say, marching over to the spot on the wall where I'd left him immobilized. I run a hand over the spot.

"What is?" Mira asks.

"I left him here. Bound to the wall. He couldn't have possibly been strong enough to break free. Only another Djinni..."

"You think it was Lee?" Mira's voice is filled with unmistakable hope.

"I don't know." But I have the distinct feeling that I'm missing something important.

Besides Jered.

9

AUGUST 26, 1866

"HOW ARE YOU FAIRING WITH YOUR YOUNG MASTER?" CALDOR ASKS.

I've been on the plantation for three weeks, and this is the first opportunity we've had to speak. Otherwise, all we've done is throw each other furtive and curious glances as we pass through the endless halls. But today we sit on the swing on the colossal porch in front of the main house as the massive willow before us sways in the warm breeze.

"She is most certainly a spitfire." I conjure a glass of iced tea and offer a second to him.

"That's one way to put it," he says, accepting the beverage.

"Does her mother treat you well?" I ask, watching his throat move as he swallows down the amber liquid. His jacket is off, and his biceps bulge beneath the thin material of his shirt.

"She is a hard woman," he says, setting down the glass, unaware of my interest. "But decent, I think. At least compared to that beast you were saddled with before I retrieved you."

"Oh, it gets far worse than him. He, for all his faults, had a small mind. It's the ones that have grander imaginations that you have to look out for." I settle back into the swing and listen to the crickets sing. I like America overall, except the clothes. I hate the itchy suits I must wear in this time period. So restrictive, *and far too warm for the muggy southern summer. I suppose the women have it worse, though. Following Caldor's example, I snap, and my jacket is removed, the top buttons undone on my own shirt.*

"Taj." Caldor eyes me with heavy dark brows that shade his brilliant green eyes. "You were one of the first?"

"Yes."

"Is there any hope?" he asks, lines of worry drawn on his forehead. "I've only been here thirty years. I've despised every moment."

"Of course there's hope," I say. And I place an arm around his shoulder. "She could always die by another's hand without passing you along. Somewhere along the way, someone is bound to do so."

"You can't believe that, not if you've been here as long as I suspect. You don't strike me as a hopeless romantic to believe in such fairy tales."

I withdraw my arm.

"If you think they'll ever 'accidentally' let us go, that's what you are. I came wanting to experience life as a human, but like so many of us, I wasn't given the chance. Now I'd kill for the opportunity to go home and never look back."

"You asked my sage advice." I rise and stretch. "Be a pessimist if you like. I'll just stay a hopeless romantic."

"What is there left to hope for?" He stands and steps close, imploring me with his eyes, hungry for an answer, a reason to not go mad.

I steady myself, meeting his gaze and holding him so that I could convey the truth behind my answer.

"Every moment of pleasure, no matter how rare, is something to cherish." I take his hand in mine and press it over my heart. "Feel that? It's a wondrous thing, as is the iced tea we just drank and the feel of the breeze on our skin. They cannot take everything, so we must steal what we can."

Caldor swallows, staring into my eyes so that now I am the one who cannot look away. "The feel of your hand on mine."

We continue to stand, unwilling to move until he wrenches his gaze from mine and the spell is broken. I am still trying to wrap my head around the moment and the feelings that accompanied it when he speaks.

"How did this happen?" he blurts out, pulling me down by my arm. His grip is solid, and I stare at his hand until he releases me. But it wasn't uncomfortable. It was welcome.

"It's a long story," I answer. I prefer not to relive it.

"Please. I need to know." His look softens, and he reaches out again, taking my hand in his far more gently this time. My skin tingles beneath his touch, and a shock of anticipation causes my cock to swell against the material of my trousers in response.

I take a good hard look at the Djinni before me. Beautiful, like most of our kind. Since the truth is, it is my fault he's here, I owe it to him. So I tell him the whole sordid story. Kitra. Achan. Cephas. Lee. Mir. That should cool my arousal.

It hurts more than I thought it would. So when I get to the worst of it, I study the graceful bend of the willow instead of his face.

Weeping willow. Why does it weep? I swish a hand through the air and watch the long thin branches flip upside down, sticking straight up in the air. Is it a happy willow now? No. I think I'd call it obscene.

I let my hand relax, and the branches drop. Weeping willow sounds right. I can't force it to be something it's not.

"So," Caldor says, and I can feel him watching my face in the moonlight. "It's our blood that does it?"

I turn my head to face him and wish at once I hadn't. He's turned pale, like he's about to be sick. But I pat his knee, nod, and once again stand to stretch.

"I think it's time I retire for the evenin'." I'm getting pretty good at the accent if I do say so myself.

"You were a fool for trusting me, Taj."

I wince at his words. "Ouch. After I shared?"

Caldor stands to face me, shaking with what I assume is either rage or fear. I suppose he's realized now that I'm to blame for his predicament. Guess this means he won't be interested in a tryst. Likely no more hand-holding either.

"I have been commanded to obey your master as well," he says slowly, making a visual effort to keep his voice even.

I shrug, trying to step past him, but he moves to block me. He is tall, and we are nose to nose now. I am very aware of his broad chest pumping in and out inches from mine.

"And what is it that she's asked of you?" If I don't play along, he may never let me sleep.

"Master Charlotte wants to know how it works. How to 'spread the wealth,'

and now I must go tell her. This could mean even greater misery for both of us,
thanks to you."

He disappears in a puff of smoke, and I cough, wiping at my watering eyes.
So much for being friendly.

10

DROPPING LIKE FLIES

"I can't believe you lost the human," Mira's voice is shrill, grinding against my nerve endings and making me wince.

"I wouldn't have lost him if you'd have stayed." Staring at the empty wall seems like the right move, though I know it won't really help.

"Now what?" Mira asks, stepping in front of my view of the wall.

"Do you think Lee took him?"

"Why would she? What would Kitra want with—" Mira stops. Her eyebrows lift. "Achan."

"Shit." I grab Mira's arms. "We need to get over there, Mir."

"But if Lee's alive, then who did we feel die?"

None of this makes sense, but I don't have time to sit and figure it out. Achan could already be taking Jered's body. Lord knows he was none too happy about being trapped inside Cephas. I throw my hands up, rematerializing outside Kitra's island fortress. Mira pops in seconds later.

"You can't just go charging in, Taj. She'll have securities in place."

"He can't have Jered," I cannot bring myself to say more. But the muscles tighten up and down my arms, my neck, and my jaw.

"Together then." Mira places a hand on my shoulder.

We thread fingers together and concentrate. Space moves around us, until we are inside the fortress, outside the throne room. Things are grander than we left them. I can see Lee's been busy redecorating on Kitra's orders. Heavy metal weapons line the walls all the way to the top. The unnatural combination of fifty feet worth of rock and metal has always made me uneasy. On the ground, suits of armor are interspersed between Kitra's marbleized victims.

Mira nods, and we go invisible to all but each other, and then, linking hands, we step right through the rock wall into Kitra's nest. My heart thumps in my chest, and my breath speeds up. Mira squeezes my hand, but that is somewhere very far away. Because in front of me, I see not one, but three thrones, each set on its own dais. Kitra sits in the center, between Cephas's body and an unknown magician with dark-red hair and a face of stone. Each holds the end of a chain that coils along the floor, ending at a thick metal collar fastened around Lee's neck.

Lee lies on the ground, head hung down. I can feel the traces of lead they've woven in the collar and chains. Enough to cause discomfort but leave her functional for whatever magic they need. At least for the next decade, until it poisons her so thoroughly, she won't be able to stand the smallest amount in a hundred-yard radius. That's how it is with Djinn. The lead builds in our systems, growing worse and worse with exposure.

Cephas—Achan?—grunts and yanks on his chain, causing Lee to slide across the floor to his feet. I cannot take another moment, and from the look on Mira's face, I know we have to move before I lose her completely.

I tug her hand, and we appear before the others, each throwing our free hand out, and knocking both the stranger and Cephas across the room into the walls, where they slump to the ground unconscious.

I smile coolly at Kitra, who grips the edges of her seat with fear. She knows that two to one means it's over. I'm going to enjoy this.

Mira lifts her hand, as though she is about to hurtle a fireball at her old master, when it hits us at the most unwelcome time, the pain that can only mean another death. It slices through my chest, and we both crumple to the floor, gripping our hearts.

I watch helplessly as Kitra's gaze darts between the two of us and Lee, who is now twitching on the floor as well. I know what she's thinking. She must have seen Lee react this way already once today. She knows how long it lasts, and she will seize the opportunity.

I can do nothing as Kitra conjures lead chains over us. One pain subsides, leaving another in its wake. *Fight, goddamn you!* My breath comes fast and hard as I glance at Lee, so broken on the ground. Mira, who looks like a ghost. I wasn't there when I should have been to stop them before. I have to do something this time.

Kitra laughs as though she knows what I'm thinking. I hear the other magicians stir. The pain is growing worse, searing my flesh. A thousand years ago, I was terrified of the sensation of so much pain. Now, because of Kitra, I am accustomed to it.

With a cry I did not know was inside me, I use the strength of my mortal body to pull the chains off Mira. I fling them with every ounce of muscle I possess. Human adrenaline. They fly at Kitra, knocking her down.

Mira crawls away from the lead and disappears with one agonizing glance at me. And I collapse back to the floor, still trapped beneath my own bonds.

My shoulders quake from both exertion and the flood of pain that slices through my skin. I did *something*.

Just not enough.

11

SLAVE

"You think you've accomplished something?" Kitra asks.

I bow at her feet, unable to move. The familiar choking of the collar cuts into my neck. I wear an onyx this time. Black. Fitting.

"She will be mine too, you will see. I might have been more lenient with you, Taj. But now, I'm going to have to be just as careful as I am with Leela here."

She's been lecturing for an hour already. Telling me how each of them has an onyx to bind me. How they'll rule the world. Blah blah blah. My brain's been working on the information I have. What I can't figure out is what happened to Jered.

"You will stay near us at all times unless commanded otherwise. You will not speak any words that may bring us harm. You will address us with the proper respect."

I don't really have to listen. My body will automatically obey. Poor Lee. What have they done to her? She sits there, expressionless.

"Master," I interrupt. She's likely to beat me anyway. I might as well try. "What's wrong with her?"

Kitra's eyebrows lift. Her gaze slides over to Lee and back. I remain impassive, waiting for her to strike, hoping she won't. She does enjoy talking. Gloating.

"Nothing," she says. "She's finally behaving appropriately, as a slave should. Of course, I had to command her not to show any emotion that might be displeasing to us. To speak only when commanded or to show us respect. To do nothing unless asked."

My blood boils. Power builds at my fingers, but I quiet it as best I can. It won't help. And neither can I, if she becomes as restrictive with me. I can see she's considering it. I remain impassive. Unblinking. Subservient. She's taken everything from Lee, everything that makes her a person. She must be screaming inside the prison that is her body.

I have to help her. Bide my time. I can do nothing for her now despite how I ache to torture the evil woman before me.

"Do you disapprove?" Kitra asks softly. She is baiting me. I will not take it. I know how to play her game.

"You are the master. I am the slave. I have no opinion that matters."

"Very good." She laughs, relaxing back in her seat.

I cannot look at Lee, though. I know I would see nothing but her wide green eyes. Empty. *Wait—I saw her react in my apartment. When she saw Jered.* But how is that possible? She cannot break the command. It is literally impossible. Isn't it? Maybe she hadn't received the command yet. But even Jered noticed the empty expression on her face.

"Feed me grapes," Kitra commands.

I rise, conjure grapes, and begin popping them into her mouth as I think.

"You too," the stranger barks.

Lee rises and begins mimicking me with him. He pulls her into his lap, drawing his lips over her fingers each time he takes one. Running his hands up her sides.

I tense, but continue my task. Who is this man that Kitra has taken him as an equal? Did she merely need three because that is stronger than two? And what does Achan think of his Leela being used this way?

Glancing at my old master's body, I see lust written all over his face. He licks his lips hungrily, watching them, but there is something in his eyes that does not feel right.

Kitra sees me watching. "You are wondering about Achan?" She laughs, grabbing my wrist to prevent me from feeding her the grape in my hand. "That is Achan," she says, pinching my cheeks, her sharp crimson nails sinking in, drawing beads of blood, to guide my gaze to the stranger now kissing Lee. "The other is Cephas. Or what's left of him."

My mouth is suddenly very dry. As if to prove it, Cephas bellows a sound somewhere between a trumpet and a lion, and Achan disentangles from Lee to look up.

"You cannot have her. I am using her right now."

I'm going to be sick.

"Now, now, boys. We have to share. At least until we possess dear Mira again." Kitra stands. "Cephas, you may have Taj for the moment."

I move obediently over to my old master's side, where I begin feeding him grapes. I don't know if that is his wish. In fact, I'm pretty sure it isn't. But grunt is not one of the languages I understand.

Achan stands, scooping Lee into his arms. The chains around her neck drop off and land on the ground with a *clank*.

"Leaving?" Kitra asks.

"For now," he says, carrying her from the room.

I desire to kill him. The fury seeps into the grape between my fingers, and the fruit explodes into pulp just as I pop it into Cephas's maw.

"Mmmm…" Cephas grunts.

Apparently, he liked it.

"Isn't that sweet?" Kitra says, joining us on Cephas's dais. "You're worried about her, aren't you, Taj? Answer."

"Yes, Master."

"Achan is too weak to truly cause her pain. Likely he is safest for her." Kitra doesn't see how much this will hurt Lee? Is she truly that blind? "Perhaps you'd like to stand guard? Just to be sure?"

She runs a hand down my arm. I do not pause or comment. Power surges beneath my skin, but I control it because I know I cannot cause her harm, no matter how much I yearn to.

"Go watch them. Report back to me. Tell me what commands he gives his pet." I fix my eyes straight ahead as I pop out of the room and into what I assume are Achan's quarters.

He is pushing through the door, Lee still in his arms, lying passively as he kisses her. I stay invisible as he sets her on the bed and stands back.

"You may talk with me, Little One. You may also feel."

Lee immediately bursts into tears, throwing her face into the cushions, her body quaking with the intensity of it. I long to touch her. Achan is the one to do so, however. He sits beside her and runs a hand down her back.

"Stop crying, Little One." I'm not sure if he's doing it to be cruel or because he did not expect it and doesn't know what to do.

She quiets and sits up, hiccupping slightly. Fear is in her eyes.

"That wasn't quite the feeling I meant," he whispers, rubbing his thumb over the tears still staining her cheek. She remains silent.

"Haven't you missed me?" he asks, scooting in closer to her, kissing her neck.

"I love Jered," she says. It is the first I've heard her speak. Her voice is quiet, but her words cut like a blade.

Achan stiffens, and his grip on her face tightens.

"So you feel nothing when I do this?" he asks, drawing her in for a kiss. She squeezes her eyes shut, gripping the blankets on the bed, until he pulls away to wait for her response.

"I feel repulsion," she spits.

He throws her onto the bed and stands, pacing with the back of his hand pressed to his mouth. I swallow my barely controlled rage. My body trembles with it. If only I had my own wish granter who would allow me to squeeze the life from this man for the final time.

"You will enjoy it," Achan says, his face twisted. "You will feel pleasure from only my touch."

Lee is silent for a moment. Then, "You cannot command this. I do not have the power."

"I can ask the others to help me," he says.

"I will still hate you inside."

"Shut up!" he screams at her, and she goes mute, cringing back on the bed. "Beg me to kiss you," he commands after a moment. "Pretend you like it. Perhaps then you will learn to. In time."

"Kiss me. Please." Her eyes glisten with unshed tears.

"You can do better than that." Achan stands above her.

She climbs to her knees on the mattress and reaches for his arms to guide him to her side. "Please, Achan." She leans her forehead against his. Nuzzles his nose. Parts her lips.

"Kiss me," she says, speaking directly over his mouth.

Everything inside me is screaming. Tears of frustration pour from the corners of my eyes. I want to leave, to shut my eyes, to kill him. But I cannot do a damn thing.

Thank the gods Mira can.

She appears over Achan's shoulder as he kisses Lee passionately, pulling her hard to him. Mira shakes her head and hits him with a bolt of energy that might have killed him.

"Oh, God," Lee says, pressing a hand to her mouth.

"No. Just me," Mira says. She digs in his pockets for the stone, but Lee intercepts her.

"It won't matter. You have to listen, Mira. They each have a stone. They combine their powers like us. That's how they did it. I'll still be bound. They have Taj, and they're coming for you next."

Mira glances at Lee's hands, which have grasped her wrists tight. Lee relaxes upon seeing her reaction and presses her head into her palms instead.

"I want to die," she says.

"I will kill him."

"That won't help. I...I just want to die."

"We will get you out, Lee." Mira sits beside her and puts an arm around her shoulders. Lee hesitates and then throws herself into Mira's chest, still unable to cry.

At least she can feel.

12

AUGUST 30, 1866

"TAJ, YOU WILL ACCOMPANY ME TO A SMALL GATHERING TODAY." CHARLOTTE presses a kiss to my cheek and trails her hand down to mine to lead me out of her chambers.

I've been wary since my conversation with Caldor. I thought I'd gotten through to the girl. She's been so...sweet since our delightful meeting. She hasn't asked for much. She's been brought up with everything she could ever want at her beck and call. I've come to realize that I was the perfect birthday gift, if only because I was probably the only thing she did not yet possess.

All she really asks for is an ear, someone to listen to her inane prattling about the various suitors available to her, and whether this girl or that was spreading rumors behind her back. She has so little substance, it is a wonder she hasn't dispersed on the breeze and floated away altogether.

"Where are we going?" I ask, as she leads me out the back door and down the sweeping steps.

The broad fields filled with rows of cotton and the surrounding woods make the ideal backdrop against the cerulean sky. Charlotte pulls me toward the woods, looking around to be sure no one has seen us. I suppose it would look inappropriate for the two of us to disappear into the semisecluded forest without a chaperone. Though I can't imagine any servant daring to question the Widow Wilde, let alone mention such a thing.

"We are going to the old gazebo in the clearing."

"I see." I try not to reveal the sense of foreboding rising inside me. "And why would we be going there in our Sunday best?"

She laughs freely, still tugging me along behind her. "I think it is time for you and some of my friends to truly get to know each other."

I follow her through the overgrown path, beneath the canopy of trees. The sun streams through the cracks, shooting long beams of yellow that mark the way like thin bars of light. I am mesmerized by the sound of mockingbirds and the humid air that makes my hair stick to my forehead. Fascinating.

The gazebo comes into view soon enough, though we appear to be the first to make it. Initially it looks like a pristine cylinder of white in the picturesque center of a field filled with wild flowers. But as we draw closer, it becomes clear that the paint has long ago begun to chip and flake, leaving bare spots of rotting wood beneath. The wild flowers aren't really all flowers. Some are. The tiny blue ones that are so vivid my eyes cannot seem to focus for too long on any single one. But those have been overtaken by the yellow-headed weeds that at first glance I thought were pretty.

"Nice place," I say, coming to a stop halfway through the field.

"We need to go to the gazebo."

"Why?"

"Do it."

My legs move of their own accord, as I have become so unused to being given such a direct order. Charlotte fingers the amulet around her neck. I swallow the moment I set foot on the first wooden step. I feel it. The uncomfortable prickle of lead. I glance around, searching for the source, but see nothing.

Still I grow weaker by the moment, and the heat suddenly seems stifling. I wipe at my forehead with the back of one hand and grasp for the railing to keep from falling over.

I scream, clutching the hand that touched the rail like I've stuck it inside the fireplace.

"You might not want to touch it," says Charlotte. "The lead's in the peeling paint."

I stare at her in disbelief.

"You should still be able to perform some magic for me. And all I really need is one thing."

"Master Lottie," I say. It is what I've become accustomed to calling her. Condescending at first. Now familiar. "What have I done?"

"Oh, my poor dear Taj," she says, sauntering up onto the platform to join me and stroking my face. "You mean besides humiliating me that first day?"

I am having trouble forming words.

"Now. I have some people I'm going to need you to gather here before you can no longer function."

13

PRICE

Lee recovers enough to sit back and grasp Mira's arms once again. "You have to help Taj. I can't bear the thought that I've done this to him."

No, Mir. Help Lee.

"Please," she says with those damn big eyes of hers.

"Okay. Help me find his stone."

They both search Achan's body until they find the stones. Mira crushes them, and I believe I feel the choker loosen a fraction of an inch. Mira conjures a dagger, but Lee stays her hand.

"No. Give him fakes. Let him believe he still controls us."

"You and your grand plans," Mira says.

"Seriously, Mir. If they find him before you finish freeing us, it could mean disaster."

"Fine." Mira conjures two fake stones. A diamond and an onyx, which she examines before replacing it in his pocket. "Now we must separate the others."

"How?" Lee asks, eyes wide.

"Go to them. Tell them Achan commanded you to go to Cephas now that he's finished with you."

Lee's face turns white. Mira's struck a much greater nerve than she knows.

"You have to control your emotions, Lee. They'll know something's up otherwise."

Lee nods, taking a deep breath. Focusing. "For Taj," she says, and I want to tell her "no."

She leaves the room, and Mira presses the dagger into the skin at Achan's neck. But she holds and then disappears. Oh no. My command. I review her words as I pop back in front of Kitra's feet.

Tell me what commands he gives his pet. Fine. She need not know about Mira then.

Lee is kneeling at Cephas's feet. "Master has sent me to you. He says he is finished for now. It is your turn." Her face contorts with terror as Cephas pulls her up by her hair. She never was a very good actress.

"What's this?" Kitra asks, standing.

"Master," I say quickly. "Achan has commanded her to feel."

Lee's eyes meet mine. She knows now that I was there. I do not move.

"Ah." Kitra sits back down. "I see how that may have been...beneficial. Very well. Cephas?"

He grunts in response.

"Leela, you may continue to feel for Cephas."

Cold bitch. I hope Mira does kill her this time. If she doesn't, I will.

Cephas throws Lee over his shoulder and takes off for his own chambers, I suppose. Mira better be quick.

I take another chance. I circle slowly behind Kitra's throne and rub at her shoulders slow and deep. She leans into me, melting beneath my touch. I continue to massage her, wishing I could tighten my fingers about her throat.

The breath on the back of my neck lets me know Mira is there. Half a second later, Kitra is blasted to the floor, head beneath Mira's foot.

"Bitch."

"Couldn't agree more," I say. "Go to Lee."

Mira looks up at me, already holding my stone in her hand. She crushes it.

"I have to find hers," she says, surprised.

"Mir. Go. NOW."

She nods and disappears, and I begin searching Kitra for Lee's stone.

Where is it? Kitra's eyes flutter open just as Mira appears with Lee in tow. She holds both stones, which she crushes with a smile.

My collar falls from my neck onto Kitra's stomach.

"I am not free." The desperation in Lee's voice tears me apart from inside. I haven't found it. I will.

"Hold on," I say.

"Kill her!" Mira screams at me. Of course. That will end it. Kitra's eyes flash with panic as my fingers really do tighten around her neck.

Pain once again twists through my chest, and I topple down on top of her, writhing. I hear the others thud beside me. Not now. Not another death. Both thoughts swim through despite the slicing inside me.

Kitra laughs, sliding out from beneath me. I see her pull a lead pipe out of nothing. She raises it up to strike, but somehow Lee's managed to move through the pain. She throws herself over me, taking the blow to her back.

"No!"

"Go," she mouths in my face, just as the pain lifts. Mira grasps my hand, and I find myself being tugged through space, to my apartment where I fall to my knees.

"No!" The glass in the window bursts into a million shards at my fury.

"Taj, we had to leave."

"We could have done it. We were so close." I fall to the floor, hands over my head.

Mira places a gentle hand on my back and speaks softly. "Taj. Lee is alive. We know that now. She will be fine. We have to find out what is happening. Three Djinn in a matter of hours?"

"She will not be fine. She is not *fine*." I stand, pulling away from her to cup my face in my hands. How could I not have found it? How could I not have killed her? I had ached for her blood the entire time I was there. What stopped me when I had the chance?

"Jered, Taj." Mira's words both bring me back into focus and answer my silent question. Has Jered had such a big effect on me?

"How would Lee feel if she came back to find him gone?" Mira squeezes my shoulder.

I try to calm myself. "He had to be there—"

"No. I searched. That's what took me so long. He was not on that island. Not him and not his body. Not even in a statue."

"Then where?"

Mira places a hand over her heart in answer. Her eyes grow wide.

"No." But I know she's right. This is about the other Djinn. Adia. Sophie's vision. Whoever it was, he had my address, and judging by the three Djinn that died in a matter of hours when no one has in a thousand years, I don't think he's helping free us. No, he came for *me* and found Jered. And Jered couldn't do anything about it. He was bound to my wall. A sitting duck.

"What do we do?" Mira asks.

"I need to get something," I say, changing into my customary jeans and T-shirt. Then I snap my fingers, and Sophie appears in front of us.

It's almost unnerving how she barely reacts despite being torn from her home in an instant.

"You needed to get a child?" Mira asks, exasperated.

"Hello," Sophie says.

"I'm going to remove the block on your memories, darling," I tell her and then snap.

Her tiny mouth rearranges into an O as she looks at me. Tears spring to her eyes. I promise myself I will fix these painful memories as soon as I can. But I need her to know as much as possible. I don't have time to explain. Not when the Djinn are dying so quickly.

I fill in Mira on Sophie's vision. And Sophie on Lee and Jered's status, the PG version anyway.

"Three?" she asks, clearly frightened.

"So far," I confirm. I look at Mira. "At least we know Brolach's okay."

"Where is he?" Mira's eyes cloud with confusion.

"He crossed back over before I came for you."

"No, he didn't." She shakes her head. "I was close to the veil. I would have felt him arrive."

I stand. "I think we've found our main suspect. Either that or he's been taken." I'm not sure which is worse. Why is it always the pretty ones that are the bad guys?

14

SOPHIE'S HELP

"WE HAVE TO HELP LEELA," SOPHIE SAYS.

"She'll kill me if Jered isn't safe first," I say. I beg her to understand with my eyes, knowing how crazy it is to feel I need the approval of a nine-year-old.

"We have to save them both," she agrees, nodding her little head, jaw set with clear determination.

"Have you seen anything else?" I kneel to look her in the eye.

"No." She averts her gaze, and all I get are lashes kissing her chubby cheeks.

"Are you frightened?" I ask, tilting her chin up to face me.

"I feel safe with you, Taj. You're my hero." She throws her arms around me, and I squeeze right back.

"Aw. How cute. Can we please get on with this?" Mira juts a hip out with impatience.

"We need to explore your vision," I say, standing. I am giving voice for the first time to the idea that's been forming in my mind.

"How?" Mira takes a step forward, reaching her hands out like she was about to grab me but thought better of it.

"Well, if they can do it, and we can do it, why not combine our powers with hers?" I search Mira's face with anticipation. Now that I've given voice to it, it feels less absurd.

"What? Why waste our time with them? Her power is nothing compared to ours." Mira snorts, turning away.

I ignore her protests and focus on convincing her. "When we did the locator spell for Lee—"

"Yeah, that was worthwhile."

"Mira, stop. Think. I felt Jered's power tugging at ours. He was helping." I grasp her arm and turn her back toward me.

"Like a flea on a horse. It was an irritation, nothing more. A way for him to help his love."

"Maybe not." I grab both her arms now in an attempt to force her to see what I see. Know what I know. "Not in Sophie's case. She's special, Mir."

Sophie beams at me and blushes in an adorable way beneath her blond bangs. I wink.

"I'll help any way I can," she says, stepping up to join our intimate little circle. Mira sighs.

"Everyone take hands," I instruct. Mira does it, but not without staring me down first. "Sophie, focus on your vision. We will be there too."

Sophie closes her eyes, and I concentrate our energy on her mind, flowing along her thoughts. A picture emerges from the chaos, focusing like a telescope until I feel like I'm standing in the corner of a room. No, not a room. A basement. Metal stairs lead up from the area opposite. The floor is concrete, spots of dirt and rust smudged into the surface. A single dangling lightbulb swings from the ceiling, casting deep shadows along all the walls. Mira and Sophie are with me, still holding my hands.

"This isn't it," says Sophie in alarm. She nearly drops my hand, but I hold tight to our connection, wanting to understand what we are seeing.

"This is different?"

"Yes. This isn't the place where he took Adia from. This is different." She looks around, wide-eyed.

"Our power added to yours must be allowing us to see what is happening now." I tighten my grip on her hand, afraid of what she might bear witness to. "Just keep focusing."

The room floods with sound and smell. Not pleasant either. Dripping water echoes against metal pipes, and something rotten makes me gag. Not good at all. The door above crashes against the wall, and footsteps clang down several steps and then pause. Sophie tenses, squeezing my hand with all her might.

"Remember, this isn't real. It's like a movie," I say, and she relaxes a tiny bit.

I strain to see through the shadows above the bottom stairs, but I can make out nothing from our vantage point. I am about to try to move us forward, when something hurtles down the remaining steps, crashing at my feet. Sophie screams.

It's a body. A woman from the looks of it, though the head is covered in a black hood. She's wearing a tank top and jeans, and her wrists and ankles are bound with rope. A tattoo of a shooting star decorates the inside of one arm. I stare openmouthed until I see her fingers twitch, and something black pokes through beneath the bonds.

She's alive. But she cannot be Djinn. How could she remain bound with simple rope? She certainly isn't a magician though. I see no aura surrounding her.

I tug at Mira and Sophie, pulling them forward, around the figure on the ground. There have to be more answers here.

I stop abruptly when I hear a faint moan, almost causing Mira to trip. She starts to protest, but I shush her, listening hard. It seems to be coming from behind the stairs. I guide us over toward the darkness and concentrate on the lightbulb until it pulls as far toward the stairs as its chain will allow. It works. Four pairs of feet become visible, three lie askew, as though their owners are either asleep or worse. The last wears familiar Nikes that are pressed into the ground, bent as far away from the others as possible.

"Jered!" Sophie calls. She drops my hand to run to her brother, and the room disappears into a swirl of color and mist.

We are back in my apartment.

"What the hell?" Mira asks, grasping the edge of the counter for support.

Sophie runs for the bathroom.

"He has Jered. I'm willing to bet those other three near him are the dead Djinn," I say under my breath, so that Sophie cannot hear.

"And who was the woman?" Mira stares at me, hard to read.

"Another victim?" I guess.

"Why bother with a human?"

"I don't think she's human," Sophie says from the doorway.

"Then what—" Mira starts.

"She's Djinn like you," Sophie says. "Couldn't you see it?"

Mira and I exchange a look. "See what?"

"The stone." Sophie focuses on the air between her hands, and a milkshake appears.

"I'm sure I would have seen a choker," Mira says.

"It wasn't a choker. It was a bracelet." Sophie pauses to draw on the liquid ice cream in her hand. "The same kind of black ribbon with a pearl in the center."

"But that's impossible," I say, forcing a smile. Then I remember the black poking through the ropes around her wrists. I'd looked away after. Could that have been the same thing as our chokers? I touch my throat.

"What if that's how he's doing it?" Mira paces before me. "What if he's enslaving his own people and killing them?"

"It doesn't make any sense. Why? What purpose could he have? And why take Jered?"

"Does it matter?" Mira stops in front of me and takes my hands in hers.

"No," I say, after a moment's thought. "No. We need an address. We need to find him. Now."

We both look at Sophie, who is slurping the last of her milkshake. The colors in her aura are dim. She rubs at her eye with a fist, and I note the dark circles underneath.

"We have to wait until she's ready," I say, recanting despite the urgency in my gut. "She can't possibly manage that kind of magic right now. Look at her."

"She has to." Mira scoffs. "You're the one who insisted we needed to work with her. You were right, and now you want to forget it?"

"No." My word rings out firm, and Mira jolts, clearly taken aback. But I will not sacrifice or endanger Sophie. Not for Jered. Not for anyone.

Mira does not press the matter. Perhaps my decisive tone has gotten the message through.

"I want to," Sophie says, making her cup disappear. "Jered needs me."

"I'm going to send you home to get some sleep," I say, looking out the window at the crescent moon hanging in the inky black night. I hadn't realized how late it had gotten.

"No!" Her little face contorts in what looks to be the ultimate tantrum.

I hold up a hand and speak. "I'm going to fix your memories again."

"No! Taj, I don't want you to. I don't want you to take them away." She starts to cry, stomping her foot, and I hesitate.

"You are no longer my master," I say.

"I don't want to be your master!" she screams. "But don't treat me like your slave either. I want to keep my memories. Shouldn't I get to decide that?"

"I can't believe she's only nine," Mira says under her breath.

Sophie looks mutinous. I lower my hand.

"Fine. But you will not be able to look again until morning, when you've recovered some energy."

"But—"

"I'll help you get some sleep," I say. She opens her mouth to retort, and I cut her off. "Don't push it."

Her mouth snaps shut, and I wave a hand, sending her to her bed and putting her to sleep.

15

BROLACH

"JERED WILL DIE IF WE DO NOT FIND HIM. NOW," MIRA SAYS.

"Since when do you care about the human?" I ask, suppressing a smirk. I know I can only push Mira so far.

"I thought he was important to you!" She throws her hands up in exasperation.

"He's important to Lee. Ergo, he's important to me." I admit what I can, though I focus on a cup of fresh coffee I've conjured instead of looking her in the eye.

"I see."

I risk a glance and find her amused and nodding. "What's that look?"

"What look?"

I am about to actually lose my cool when Brolach's handsome face appears millimeters from mine. I flip my hand up, and he is immediately thrown into the same wall I left Jered stuck to.

"What?" he squeaks. I try to ignore how adorable he sounds and squeeze my fist together, choking him.

"Taj!" Mira screams, grabbing at my arms.

"Where's Jered?" I don't take my eyes off him.

"He can't answer you if he can't breathe," Mira hisses through clenched teeth.

This time I really do glance at Mira, who has given up tugging at me and stands with her arms folded, glaring instead. I loosen my grip, and Brolach slides to the floor, gasping.

"We're watching you," I say. "Make one move, and—"

He starts crying. "I...I wanted to check on you because...because of the deaths...I was worried. I thought maybe..." The tears flow louder and faster.

Mira rolls her eyes and goes to help him to his feet. "You'll have to forgive Taj here, Brolach. He seems to think you're a serial killer. He tends to jump to conclusions. It's that hot head of his."

Brolach quiets and looks at me with those huge green puppy-dog eyes. "You think I did that?" He goes so white, I think he's going to faint.

"You fit the description of the killer," I say in my defense. "And you disappeared shortly before the first murder."

"How do you know what the killer looks like?" he asks, sounding nothing more than curious.

"Ignoring the whole you disappeared part, I see," I point out. He winces. "Fine. We have information from the vision of a magician that says the killer is a male Djinni about your size."

"Your sister's friend saw this?" he asks, backing up to his feet.

"That isn't your concern. What is your concern is that I am losing patience. And when I lose patience, I tend to get a bit impulsive"—I lean in—"and nasty."

"I didn't do it!" he yells. "Why won't you believe me?"

"Why don't you start by telling us where you were?" Mira suggests, stepping between us.

He swallows, looking from one of us to the other.

"We know you didn't pass through the veil," Mira prompts. "You lied."

"But I did!" He's crying again. "I did."

"I would have felt you." So much for being a hothead. Mira seems to believe me now.

"No. I was there for only a moment. I was looking for Rachim."

"Clearly you are having trouble with the concept of truth." I clench my fists. "Saying you are going back and staying for seconds does not qualify."

"Oh. I wish I understood the human rules better. It hurts when I get it wrong." Brolach rubs at his throat again and slumps his shoulders.

"Explain yourself," Mira says.

"I wanted to find Rachim, to tell him what it was like. Being here. With you." He looks directly over Mira's shoulder at me with those big eyes again. He has very long dark eyelashes. Very pretty.

"Who is Rachim?" I rub at the ache in my forehead.

Mira responds from beside me. "Another Djinni. Huge proponent of closing the veil between the worlds permanently."

"I enjoy debating the issue with him," Brolach says, working his way to a standing position. "He almost had me convinced until—" His mouth snaps shut, eyes cast downward.

"Until what?"

"Until I met you." He says it so quietly I can barely hear him.

It's a nice line, but if I were convinced that easily by a pair of pretty eyes, I'd have learned nothing in the last thousand years.

"You didn't find him when you crossed over?" Mira taps her chin. "I don't remember feeling him either, actually."

"No. So I decided to search this side. Unfortunately, that's when the first pain hit. And I've looked all over and cannot find him."

"This world is a big place." I peer through my fingers, forgetting about the headache.

"I thought he might have been in one of the places he's mentioned in our talks." Brolach straightens his T-shirt and brushes off his pant legs.

Shock ripples through me, and I let my arms drop to my sides. My mind is blown. "You mean the guy who wants to close off access to the human world likes to vacation here?"

"Oh, not vacation, no." Brolach chuckles. "He says that if he doesn't experience this world, he would have no right to make such decisions."

"I see." I fold my arms over my chest. "Very sporting of him."

"He's been careful to keep track of all those who've crossed over to stay. He's really quite organized." Brolach sits on the leather sofa, hands in lap.

"Wait—*what*?" My outburst causes him to stand again like he's accidentally sat in a fire pit.

"He's been careful—"

"Why would he do that?"

"*How* would he do that?" Mira asks over me.

Brolach shrugs, playing with his long fingers. "He has followers that help him watch the curtain. I've kept watch myself once or twice. You said yourself you can feel when others cross if you're right there."

"The fucker has a list of Djinn." I make eye contact with Mira.

She nods, eyes wide.

"Brolach, we have to stop him." I place my hands on his shoulders. "But we also have to retrieve Leela."

"You mean your sister?" He glances between Mira and me.

"Yes, that's right. With your help, it should be no problem."

"Of course I'll help! I broke a human rule and lied. I have to make it up to you." He bounces in place with a brilliant smile, which I return. It seems likely the culprit is his friend, Rachim. So no harm done.

"Then it's time we repay an old debt." My fury reignites beneath the surface. I find emotion a good way to channel my power, and rage is a strong one.

"I don't know if this is a good idea." Mira's hand is on my shoulder again, caution in her voice.

"What? Why not?"

She comes around to look at me face-to-face, cupping my cheeks. "Taj, Lee is suffering, but think about it. She will still be there tomorrow. A hundred years from now, we will know where to find her. But Jered is human. Frail. What would she want?"

"I can't stand the thought of them hurting her. She's paid enough, Mir." My chest tightens at the certainty of her suffering.

"Taj." Mira drops a hand to my shoulder and with the other one smooths my hair back from my face. "We should stay together. Power in numbers. We can't afford to charge in there again unprepared."

I hesitate, closing my eyes and breathing out slowly through my mouth. I could have killed Kitra, and for whatever reason, I did not. Now Lee is paying the price. Gods know what they're doing to her right now. But Mira is right. Jered is in mortal danger. So are the other Djinn. And if another one dies at the wrong moment...

"It's your call, Taj."

"Jered," I say, opening my eyes again.

Mira smiles, and I feel Brolach slip his hand tentatively in my own. I squeeze it, and he relaxes. Mira closes the circle, and we are connected.

"Where do we find Rachim?" I shake out my hair that Mira messed with.

"Can we track him?" Mira asks.

"Not without something of importance to him. Or a vision like Sophie's."

"Sophie?" Brolach asks, and I tense, realizing my mistake in using her name. I will protect her at all costs.

"She cannot help tonight, and I fear tomorrow will be too late." He needs to know no more.

Mira taps her foot. "What we need is his list."

"Brilliant!" I say. "Brolach?"

"The list of Djinn who've passed through the veil?"

"Yes."

He seems to steel himself. "Okay. I can do that."

"We're coming with you."

He smiles, grateful. Obviously, he doesn't get that I still feel I must keep an eye on him. But I give him a little kiss to relax him, and we're off.

16

AUGUST 30, 1866

I HATE BEING THE CENTER OF ATTENTION. OKAY, THAT'S NOT ENTIRELY TRUE. *I hate being the center of attention when I am weak. So lying in the middle of a gazebo with peeling lead paint surrounded by four humans is not high on my list of ideal situations. Yet here I am. Such is my life.*

"It's starting to burn through my clothes," I say, trying unsuccessfully to twist my body into a more comfortable position. "So unless you want me naked, you better get a move on."

Charlotte's laugh rings in my ears, and her cohorts join in right along with her. They look at her like a queen. Like the others used to look at Kitra. With a combination of fear, hatred, and respect.

Her admirers are all male. Three that I've seen in her group before. Charles Demonte, Pierce Thomas, and Lucas Caroby. All three quite attractive. Or at least they were before they decided to gather around my writhing body to laugh.

I know they've all been competing for Charlotte's affections. All from wealthy Southern families. All the subject of many a tiring one-way conversation in Charlotte's rooms at night. But what they are doing here is beyond me.

"You see, Taj, we have a deal. Charles, Lucas, Pierce, and me. If I share my power with them, they will help me inherit this land and run it on my own. You were right," she says, leaning down to whisper in my ear. "I've tried relations,

but sexual manipulation only goes so far. I need something a bit more permanent."

She straightens up and speaks to her admirers. "If you want power as we have discussed, I am willing to share it with you right now. But if you do not take me seriously, and refuse to do what I say, you will suffer consequences beyond your wildest dreams."

She concentrates on her aura, forcing it out around her, bringing in a small whirlwind, kicking up the loose leaves and dirt on the gazebo floor and nearly choking me. But it has the desired effect. Her showmanship is impeccable. When the wind dies, she's dressed in a simple gossamer gown, her long blond hair flowing down her back like liquid sunshine. And in her hand is a curved dagger with a jeweled handle. But it isn't the handle that worries me—it's the lead blade.

"Pick him up," she says to the boys.

Charles and Lucas each take one of my arms and hoist me up to a standing position. Well, if you can call leaning on both for support standing. Charlotte moves toward me, pressing the flat of the blade to my cheek. My skin sizzles in response, smoke rising from the sides of the knife, and I scream. The boys nearly drop me, but she pulls it away from my face.

"We are going to need some skin for this," Charlotte says, and she focuses on a spot just below my neck. In moments, I am naked from the waist up, sweat glistening on my chest in what I doubt is a very enticing way.

At least my pants are mostly still intact. Always look at the positive.

"I do not recommend this, Master," I whisper. It is becoming painful to speak, but I must try.

"Of course you don't!" Charlotte laughs again. "You are delightful, Taj. I'm so glad to have you in my possession."

She pulls Pierce over with a yank of his arm, and he cannot seem to look me in the eye.

"Do you agree to my terms?" she asks.

He licks his lips and nods quickly. She smiles, says, "Hold him tight," and draws the blade across my upper arm. I open my mouth, but I haven't the voice for another scream.

"Drink," she says.

For a moment, I think Pierce will refuse. He is as white as marble and looks *as though he might retch. But instead, he leans forward, closes his eyes, and presses his lips to my wound. He is tentative at first, slipping the tip of his tongue along the wound, and then as he begins to actually suck on my blood, he draws on it with more fervency.*

It is more than agony. It is something like the worst kind of degradation. It is personal. And all I can seem to think is that Rhada went through this. Lee went through this. Dear gods.

I sob openly, and I continue to do so when Charlotte guides him away from my arm. His eyes are wild, his face below his nose covered in my blood. And on him is born a new aura, also blood red.

"Let him go," Charlotte orders.

Is that a quiver I hear in her voice? I sink to my knees, clutching at the wound on my arm. I hear one of the boys that held me vomiting over the side of the gazebo. I am breathing very hard and feel quite dizzy.

"Bring him away from the lead," Charlotte says. And strong hands tug below my arms, pulling me down the steps to the field of wild flowers and weeds where I roll down onto the prickly ground and stare up at the sky.

It is growing dark. The moon is out, large and round, and it throws so much light down on us that I would have hardly noticed the difference if I hadn't been staring right at it.

I am strong enough to stand now. My cut is healed, and so is my face. But I stay put, not wanting to acknowledge the idea that she brought two others here for the same purpose.

She drops to her knees beside me, and her beautiful, young face swims into view. Why?

"I'm trying to tell you something," I say. "Haven't I already proved an excellent teacher?"

I can see the blush in her cheeks, a combination of the bright moon and her fair skin.

"You are only making them more powerful by doing this," I say.

"That is the idea," she says. She is not very good at keeping her feelings hidden. I can see how I've struck a chord despite her snappy reply.

"What will you have left to barter with?" I ask.

"You. They will never be as powerful as me as long as I have you."

"And if you accidentally kill me now? Drain me? Then what?"

"*I will not. I am letting you heal between sessions.*"

"*I see. And if I do survive, but they take me from you by force?*"

"*They cannot.*" *She waves a hand in dismissal. But I can see the fear light her eyes.*

"*I will do what I can to prevent it. But how is it you think your mother acquired me?*"

Charlotte stands and turns away.

"*Back on the gazebo, Taj.*"

"*Yes, Master Lottie. If you think it wise.*"

17

SEARCH AND RESCUE

MIRA AND I HOVER NEARBY AS BROLACH APPROACHES RACHIM'S CURRENT sentry. I keep some of my essence connected to his, however. I want to hear what he says.

I am taking over next, Brolach tells the energy.

I thought Sharif was next.

She will be here after.

Very well, here is the information to pass. She glides over him, mingling with his essence, and I pull back so she does not feel me. When she separates and floats off into the distance of space, Mira and I swirl over Brolach's shapeless form.

Here is the list in its entirety, he says. Names, images, and addresses all tumble through me. Snippets of human-Djinn faces from different times. I see four others, then myself, Mira, and Lee nearly right away. The list consists of about fifty in all.

There is no need to stay, so I say no more, just pull them both back through the boundary with me, settling into my familiar human form and breathing in the cool night air that rushes in off Lake Michigan. The water helps me think.

"It is in order of who crossed over first," I say after a minute of thought.

"Yes, but all locations are updated as the information passes through. Leela is registered as being on an island in the Atlantic."

"It was adjusted already?" I ask, surprised.

"When Mira came through. She knew this information and passed it unknowingly to the sentry. That's how it works."

"Spying without others' knowledge. Rachim seems to be a real upstanding guy." I kick at the base of the sofa.

"And what did you suppose he was planning on doing with this list of his?" Mira asks, not bothering to keep the venom from her voice.

Brolach stumbles backward slightly as though the thought has pushed him off-balance. "I...I don't know. I assumed he intended to gather everyone together, or try to, before he closes the door."

"It would seem," I say, "he is using this information to collect and destroy all Djinn who've made this side of the veil their home."

Brolach starts to fall, and I catch him. I believe he's just fainted. I look at Mir, uncertain, and she rolls her eyes. Delicate constitution. I suppose we were all like that in the beginning.

I let my magic flow through him, strengthening him, and his eyes flutter open. He gasps, seeing my face so close, and I grin. I can't help but be pleased at eliciting that kind of response.

"We have to start at the beginning, because I believe that's what he's done," I say. "He came for me and found Jered instead. I was early on his list. One of the first to cross over."

"Then Lee will be next," Mira says.

And he now knows exactly where to get her. "We have to check each of the other four. See if I'm correct." Mir was right—we have to stay methodical, not go charging in making mistakes like before. I snap, and we each have a physical copy of the list to work with.

"That means we check on Ceralis, Noris, and Adia first," Brolach says, checking the paper in his hand.

"We should split up for this," Mira says. "It'll go faster."

"Fine," I say, though I feel uneasy. We will lose our strength in numbers. But Lee. Jered.

"I'll find Ceralis," Brolach says.

"I'll take Noris," Mira says.

"That leaves me Adia." It makes sense. If she sees someone unfamiliar, she'll no doubt kill them. "Stay invisible at all times," I say. "We don't know if their masters know enough to trap us on sight. Or if the Djinn themselves are friendly. Meet back here in precisely one hour regardless of what you find."

Brolach and Mira nod, though their faces couldn't be more different. Brolach's looks childlike and pale, Mira's determined and set. We all disappear.

Adia's living in luxury, of course. A penthouse over the Riviera. One sweep of the place with my senses, and I find only a magician asleep in the grand, heart-shaped bed. How tacky. Black silk sheets, mirrored ceiling.

As soon as I get a peek at him, with his lacy red eye mask, snoring in the bed, I have more trouble understanding the mirror thing. Why would he want a reminder of that? I decide to break my own rule in the interest of saving time. If I do well enough, I can move on to number four and finish by the time the others are back.

"Boo." I shake his shoulder and watch with amusement as he bolts upright in the bed, fumbling for his mask.

He's a weasely little fellow, with whiskers on his chin, and a small snoutlike nose. Yuck. So glad I didn't have to serve him.

"Who? What the—?" His beady black eyes dart around until finally settling on me. Fear creeps over his whole body as he shrinks back into the cushions. "What do you want?"

"I want Adia."

"She's gone. Left me." He's trying to sound like he's in control, but I see him shaking beneath the sheets.

"When?" I ask.

"Four days ago. I came home, and she was gone. I tried calling her back, but then I found this." He fumbles on his nightstand and holds out a black ribbon with a cracked sapphire down the center. "Freed."

"She didn't hang around to kill you then?" I ask, because I like making him tremble.

"I was a good master. Never beat her." The idea of a little nothing like him laying a hand or whip on Adia's Amazon body is ludicrous. Still, he had the power.

"Bravo." I clap slowly in mock adoration.

"I see you belong to no one." He leans forward, becoming a bit braver.

"Just myself."

"We could be good together. You're more my type, you know."

"No. I didn't know. Now I'm going to have nightmares, thank you very much." I wave a hand, and he falls back on the bed, unconscious. I debate killing the worthless scum, but decide against it. Jered would not approve. Why I care when such feelings already cost us, I don't have time to dwell on at the moment.

I access my paper for the fourth Djinni on the list. Qadira. She was last seen in Los Angeles. I snap my fingers, mostly out of habit, and appear in a small bungalow-style house in Arcadia, California. Nice, but not ostentatious. *Must be free*, I think. I begin poking around the place. Neat little kitchen. The appliances gleam like they've never been used. They probably haven't.

The living room is tidy as well, a large flat-screen mounted on the wall. The bathroom is decorated in a celestial theme. Very Djinn. I move on to the bedroom. A king-size bed is stuffed inside the tiny space, taking up nearly every square foot. The covers are mussed like she hadn't had time to make it, which does not fit with the rest of the house. The dresser drawers are open, clothes hanging out. Interesting. Some are men's. The nightstand appears empty at first. Then I see that the contents were knocked onto the floor, probably in a scuffle.

I stoop to pick up the alarm clock, now blinking twelve, and snap on the radio. R and B. I reach for the picture frame that lies facedown on the carpet and smooth my hand over the glass.

A girl smiles back. Young, of course, full of beauty and life. She's got short dark hair and the telltale emerald eyes of a Djinni. I note the shooting star tattoo on her arm and squeeze my eyes shut while the room stops spinning, the vision still crystal clear in my mind. Bound and thrown on the floor of the cold basement.

She looks so happy in this photo where she leans into the arms of a second Djinni. A man, tall and muscular with wild dark hair, emerald-green eyes, and the kind of five-o'clock shadow that makes me start breathing hard. I note the matching tattoo on his shoulder.

I straighten out my legs, setting the picture back on the nightstand. I'm thrown upward into the ceiling with such force, the breath is knocked out of me.

"Where's Dira?" His voice is as sexy as his picture suggests. Never mind that he's got me stuck to the ceiling. What I don't know is where he is on the list.

18

IMPORTANT

"I WAS JUST TRYING TO FIGURE THAT OUT MYSELF," I SAY AS COOLLY AS I CAN manage while stuck to a ceiling.

He tightens his grip on the air, choking me until I see stars, and then loosens it. "Let's try this again."

"My name is Taj. I'm looking for my friend, who I believe has been taken by the same person who took Qadira."

Handsome and Dangerous pauses while mentally reviewing this information. "Took her?" he asks, finally. His voice is choked with emotion.

"I'm sorry, I am. But I believe she's alive still. I have good reason, which I'd be happy to share if you'd be so kind as to let me down."

"How do I know you aren't the one responsible?"

"You don't. Though I'd be a pretty stupid evil mastermind to come back to the scene of the crime and get caught by the vengeful boyfriend."

A smile tugs at the corners of his very full lips, and he sets me down slowly, where I rub at my neck and swallow a few times to make sure it's all working right. I sit on the edge of the bed.

"Tell me what you know," he says.

I explain the vision. The pain. Lee and Jered. I leave Sophie out. Also the list, leaving vague the "how I tracked them down" part.

"I can't believe it's a Djinni doing this and not a human," he says and shakes his head. "You saw the tattoo, and you traced it back to the Order. Clever."

"That's right," I agree, having no idea what Order he's talking about. "Now it's your turn. Tell me what you know."

He glares at me, looming close. "First Taj, you should know that if I find out you had anything to do with Dira's disappearance, you are a dead man."

"Understood," I say, a bit turned on. "Likewise I'm sure."

"So this Jered was taken, but he isn't Djinn?" he asks, stroking his stubble and making me want to touch.

"Yes. He's a magician."

"But he freed your friend?"

"Correct. They're in 'love.'" I make quote signs with my fingers.

He laughs. "Well, I felt the deaths as well, of course. So did Dira. We knew by the third that something wasn't right." He runs his hands over his face and through his magnificent dark hair.

"We need something of hers," I say, suddenly understanding what I have to do. "So we can do a locator spell."

"Of course!" He forgets to doubt me and begins riffling through the open drawers.

"Um, I think you'll do," I say, placing a hand on his shoulder. "Let's go meet the others."

It is four minutes past the hour deadline when I appear with Dreamboat at my side. Mira pulls her hand quickly from her mouth, but not before I see she's been biting her nails.

"Where were you?" she screams at me.

"Solving all our problems. You?"

She slaps me. "You're the one that insisted we be back here on time come hell or tidal wave."

"That's high water, not tidal wave," Dreamboat interjects.

"Whatever. Taj, I thought you'd been taken. I thought Kitra or...or..."

"I'm okay, Mir," I say, pulling her into my arms, kissing her head.

She sniffles a little and then backs away, regaining her composure.

"Where's Brolach?" I ask, looking around.

"Brolach?" asks Dreamboat.

"He was helping us look," I say.

"He didn't come back, Taj," Mira says.

"What?"

"You heard me. He didn't show. Then again, neither did you." The tip of her nose is flushed, like she's been crying. I wince. Sometimes I can be a bit self-absorbed.

"We're wasting valuable time. We have to do the locator spell," Dreamboat says. I suppose I ought to ask his name. Then again, he just accused me of wasting precious time.

Mira does it for me. "Who's this?"

"Ray."

Mira stares at his hand, waiting in midair for a handshake.

I hold out my own hands in an effort to both salve the feelings in the room and get everyone back on track. Who knows how much time we have? The others accept without hesitation, forming our circle.

"This is for Qadira," I explain to Mir. "She's the one we saw in the vision."

"Sophie—" Mira starts.

"Who?" Ray asks. I glare at Mir. She clamps her mouth shut.

"Focus," I say. "We must find Qadira."

Our power flows together, blooming between our arms, and I focus on the girl at the bottom of the stairs. I find myself rushing through time and space, the only thing grounding me are the hands of the others.

We fly through the Midwest, stopping finally in Minnesota near Lake Superior. I see an old Victorian-style house, weatherworn and in bad need of a paint job. It's set apart from the other houses, resting on a large piece of overgrown property. One of the windows is broken, like someone had let a softball fly and then been too freaked out to go into the creepy old house after it.

We burst through the door, down a narrow, dark hallway and through another door, and down the familiar metal steps into the basement. This time nothing prevents us from moving into the shadows or sensing what lies beneath.

The three bodies are gone now, though a deep-crimson stain shades the ground. I smell the coppery scent of blood. Three figures sit on the floor side by side, hands bound behind their backs, black hoods over their heads. I recognize the jeans and T-shirt of Qadira. The other Djinni, or so I assume, I do not recognize them. I search the list in my memory and find the next name after ours. Charmaine. That must be him.

The aura and sneakers of the third figure are unmistakable. Jered.

He's alive.

But for how long?

19

AUGUST 30, 1866

THE LEAD'S EFFECTS OVERWHELM ME FASTER NOW. MY LEGS FEEL LIKE RUBBER AS I take the last step onto the platform. I want to reach for something to steady myself but do not want to touch the rails. The world starts to spin, and I am falling. But hands catch me from behind, and I am soon propped up once again, this time by Pierce.

His eyes looked so insane when he finished feeding, I wonder if he'll sink his teeth right into my flesh for a second course. But he stays put as Charlotte joins us.

"Charles," she calls. "You're next."

She pulls the knife out of thin air, and holding my chin so she can see my eyes, she thrusts it hilt deep into the crook between my shoulder and my neck.

"Aaah!" I scream, and a flock of birds hidden among the trees take flight.

Charlotte yanks the blade from my body, and I sink back against Pierce.

"Drink," she says, stepping aside.

Charlie steps forward, staring at the crimson liquid flowing hot and steady over my chest. He leans in and then squeezes his eyes shut, shaking his head.

"I can't do this, Lottie. This is some sort of sick witchcraft, and I cannot be a part of it. I believe the Lord Jesus would not look favorably upon it."

He rises, backs away, and flies down the steps into the night. I let out a sigh of relief. But Lucas is there in a flash, and he does not hesitate. His mouth is on my skin, and I can feel his throat moving up and down as he gulps at the wound, sucking greedily.

I hear myself moaning, but I have no more control over it than I do my own will. Then the worst of it—Pierce really does lean over and bite me. He tears at the tender skin on the other side of my throat. Buzzing sounds in my ears, and I am losing sensation in my extremities. Charlotte winds her fingers through my hair. Retribution for the lesson I tried to teach her.

I take comfort in knowing that even Charlotte Wilde cannot be immune to the pain when playing with power. She was warned.

The snapping of a twig. A gasp in the night.

"Who was that?" Charlotte asks, head snapping up like a dog sniffing for the scent of prey.

Lucas detaches from my neck, his entire front coated in my blood. Pierce drops me to the ground, where I curl up on my side.

"Find them!" Charlotte yells.

The two boys run into the trees after whoever was fool enough to spy and give himself away. Charlotte's foot blocks my view, and she pushes my head with it until I am looking up at her.

"You see, Taj? You are still alive."

Barely.

"And now I have two suitors far worthier of me than I started with."

She steps off the gazebo and sighs. "I would like to leave you here for the rest of the night. But I'm afraid I need you to find this spy and to take care of dear, dear, Charles."

She pulls on the air, hand over hand, and I slide across the splintered wood like I'm being dragged by a rope. She hauls me down the steps headfirst, bump, bump, bump. But at least I am away from the lead.

What sadistic bastard decided to mix paint with lead anyway?

"Go find the eavesdropper and then Charles, and make sure they do not reveal the truth."

"Yes, Master."

I think it's safe to say I should drop the "Lottie" now.

20

STORMING THE CASTLE

THE MOMENT WE DROP HANDS, WE NOD IN SILENT AGREEMENT. *WE GO NOW*. I push aside the nagging realization that Brolach was not among the captured. I do not want to face the possibility that I might have been played.

We arrive outside the dilapidated house in the freezing middle of the night. The first snow of the season has begun to drift lazily down from the heavens, and I shiver as I peer cautiously through the broken windowpane. I throw a sliver of blue light out from my fingers but see nothing other than the silent, depressing interior.

"Let's go." I motion to the others with my hand.

Ray pushes at the door, which creaks obligingly open. We move forward in a tight group, Mira in the center, myself at the rear. Ray leads the way to the hall door, which swings loose on its hinges. We follow his lead, floating down the steps, an inch or two above the metal, to avoid giving away our presence.

When we get to the bottom, I throw a ball of illumination to the ceiling, quadrupling the glow from the single bulb, and the place is bathed in light. We rush as one behind the steps, Ray pulling the hood off Qadira and kissing her deeply.

Mira releases the man I suspect is Charmaine, prying off his bracelet with some difficulty. But I stand uselessly to the side, rooted to the spot.

No Jered.

No. No. No. This cannot be right. He was here. I saw him. Right here. I reach a hand forward as though he might suddenly appear on the spot. He can't be far, I think. Then I realize how ridiculous that is. A Djinni could have transported him anywhere in the world if he'd wanted to.

Charmaine stands, looking from one of us to the other, and then disappears. Back through the veil, I assume. I can't blame him. Qadira rubs her wrists, now completely free, and relishing in her man's strong and steadying embrace.

"Are you all right?" Ray asks tenderly.

I push away the twinge of jealousy that suddenly attacks me. I'm the rescuer, not the rescued, I remind myself.

"I was so scared," Qadira says.

After one more kiss, Ray extracts himself and approaches me with a smile. "Taj, I don't know how to thank you. I'm sorry I accused you."

"No problem, man. I understand, believe me. Now we need to wait here for the bad guy."

He takes one agonized look at his woman and shakes his head. "I'm sorry. I really am. But we don't want any more part of this, Taj. Good luck finding your friend." He smiles, takes Qadira's hand, and they both disappear.

"Well, that's a fine how-do-you-do." Mira snorts.

"Not that different from you," I sing and instantly regret it.

"Let's leave an alarm here. We'll know when he comes back. In the meantime, we need Lee," Mira says.

"What's the rush?" I ask. "I thought you wanted to settle this first."

"We need her to locate Jered. Or did you decide he isn't worth the trouble? Either way, Lee is our priority now."

"Sure," I say, though I want to say more. I want to yell and scream and rip the house apart in the hopes of finding him. We were so close. What does the killer want with a magician anyway? Hopefully enough to keep him around. Unlike the other Djinn, we won't feel it if he dies.

I set an alarm on the front door and the basement, then take Mira's hand, and flash through space, heading for Kitra's island. We make our way back through to the door of the throne room.

"Do not rush in on your white horse, hothead," Mira says. "Let's talk it through first."

I nod in agreement, because that's the easiest way to get her to keep moving, and we enter.

Kitra sits on high, but I do not see a sign of Cephas or Achan. Lee sits at her feet, silent and blank, and my heart lurches.

"Leela," Kitra says. "How long until you think they will come for you?"

"I do not know, Master." Something in her voice frightens me. Like there is no soul behind it.

Mira squeezes my hand, but between the disappointment in not finding Jered and my seeming inability to get ahead of the threats that always come for those I love, I'm finding it hard to focus on anything more than my desire to finish what I started before our escape. All my pain is focused on Kitra. I need to kill the bitch. Now is our opportunity. We can take them out one at a time.

"We move now," I say, eyes locked on Lee.

"Taj, wait—"

"*Now.*"

I pull Mira forward and step into view. Lee raises an arm to strike, and I immobilize her against the wall. A sudden memory assaults me, and I see Lee standing frozen in the doorway, holding Mira pinned, unable to either hurt her friend or let her go. I press my cheek to my shoulder, remembering the tender kiss she gave me when I took over and saved her from herself.

Now here I stand, in much the same situation, understanding what she must have felt. The difference is, I know what has to be done to rescue her. I know she will forgive me.

Lead restraints bind her hands, and I turn to Kitra. Mira has already moved forward, gathering her energy to strike. She raises her hand, a sphere of blue lightning ready to be released, when I realize something is very wrong. Kitra is laughing, her dark eyes dancing with malice.

I spin just as Mira lets go and see them. Achan and Cephas cowering behind Brolach. My gaze rests on the choker around his neck, and time slows. I raise my hands to strike. Mira's lightning bolt bounces harmlessly off an invisible shield in front of Kitra and hits me full force from behind.

Electricity flows through my body, forcing my back to arch, my skin to light on fire. Ten times more intense than the pain of lead, I lose all muscle control instantly, falling forward to the stone floor. Buzzing sounds in my ears, and my vision blurs.

I hear Mira. "What—" Followed by her scream. And then there is only black.

21

HOW MANY DJINN DOES IT TAKE TO CHANGE A LIGHTBULB?

I COME TO WITH THE FAMILIAR CHOKING SENSATION ALREADY SQUEEZING MY neck. Shit. When will I learn to stop being so impulsive? I just can't stand sitting around watching the people I love suffer. Not that I love all that many people. But those that do mean something to me, well, I desire to protect them. What the fuck is all this power for if I can't even accomplish that much?

My head still aches from Mira's blast. I've no doubt that Kitra would be little more than a pile of ash had it hit its mark. I open my eyes, simply because I know I cannot avoid it for much longer.

I wish I could close them again. Brolach, Mira, and Lee all kneel at Kitra's throne. Achan and Cephas stand at either side of her royal evilness like silent sentries. All three Djinn are trussed up in the red-and-gold harem outfits of Kitra's choosing. If I checked, I'm sure I'd find I was already wearing it too.

I struggle my way to my feet and stumble forward toward the others. Kitra barely glances up.

"Well, look who's decided to join us. Kneel with your friends."

I do. This way the floor is closer anyway, in case I pass out again. This must be what humans feel like after drinking too much. Too bad a lightning bolt to the back isn't as fun of a way to get there.

Kitra smiles, clearly pleased at my compliance. "Finally. Four Djinn. Our power will be limitless."

None of us bother to correct her. For all intents and purposes, she's right. She can have just about anything her shortsighted little human mind can conjure.

"Join hands, my pets. That is how it works, no?"

We rise as one, creating the circle of power she seeks. I managed to delay this moment by over a thousand years. Not bad. Except that now there is one more. One more equals frightening possibilities.

Power bubbles between us. I'm pretty sure it's visible to even the magicians because Kitra's face appears ecstatic, bathed in the blue glow. I feel my eyes flash to light green and see the others are the same. As wind builds and circles around us, Mira's and Lee's hair flies up behind them.

"Let's start simple, shall we?" Kitra says. "Fix Cephas."

A small tornado of golden light swirls from the center of our circle. It grows and flies to surround the giant to Kitra's right. His face contorts with real fear, but when it lifts moments later, his eyes look sharper, and he lets out a roar, beating his chest like an animal.

Kitra's eyebrows raise. Achan steps away.

"I am back," Cephas declares in triumph.

Wonderful. It's a regular family reunion.

"Excellent," Kitra says. "Achan?"

The devil steps back into place, squaring his shoulders. I think I see what happened now. How his red hair blends with Kitra's. She found another magician of her own lineage to transfer his soul to. I wonder briefly whether I should feel bad for the boy who's been displaced. Or if he was as worthless as the rest of his family tree.

"Can you give me my original body? Make me—us—young forever without having to transfer again?"

The answer comes as one from four sets of lips. "Yes, Master."

"Do it."

While we grant his request, I think about what just happened. We all answered in unison. As one. Perhaps...

I open myself up to the others, let my own essence flow through the connection. The power. And I feel them as I brush past. I find Lee, allow myself to embrace her mind. Great sadness rushes through me, and I gasp at the intensity of the waterfall of emotion.

Lee.

Taj? I can feel you. I can speak.

Yes, darling. It is the power. The connection. We must talk quickly. Let me get the others. I reach out to the other minds in the circle, but Lee continues as though unable to stop her thoughts.

I want it to be over, Taj.

I know. We will get through this. We will find a way.

No. I can't continue. Cannot live with the fear of losing everything I am.

Don't talk like that, Lee. Mira says it.

I am vaguely aware of Kitra and the others making requests, which we automatically grant. Kitra's original body. Immortality for all. The additional palace filled with gold.

I am scared, Brolach says.

We WILL find a way out, I say.

Jered. It is a random thought from Mira, and I wish I could stop it. Lee's mind reels with even more intense despair.

Jered? she whispers.

I could not find the Djinni you sent me to seek, Brolach says. *I came back early to the apartment, and Leela was waiting for me.*

You tried your best to kill me, Lee says.

Anger swells within me, and the magic between us floods with red. The magicians take no notice.

He should have, Lee tells me. *I would have preferred it. But I had to fulfill my command. I have to bring back any Djinni I come in contact with.*

Do not be angry, Taj, Brolach pleads. *I was frightened. I did not wish this.*

Of course not, I say. *No one does.*

"...rule over the world. We will begin with more slaves. An army of magicians. Bring all the magicians here and enslave them to our will." Kitra's thinking bigger now.

The conversation ceases. I feel Lee trying to pull her hand away from mine. To break the circle. I am shocked, but I tighten my grasp, forcing her to stay put. I cannot break the command. But neither should she be able to...

The power flows outward, filling the room, lifting us from the ground and encompassing our bodies in light. I am momentarily blinded by the intensity of it. I've never felt the like. My entire being is pulled apart, flowing instantaneously around the world, plucking the swirling auras of magicians from below, depositing them in the throne room of Kitra's fortress. Each one bound to serve. Men, women, children.

Children.

Sophie. I cannot allow her to be taken. Is it too late?

NO.

My hand twitches against Lee's. Loosens. She pulls away, and my fingers slide over hers. The connection is broken. The four of us crash to the ground in a quivering heap, our individual energy nearly drained.

Kitra hardly acknowledges us. She is too busy running through the rows of fresh new slaves she's just acquired.

"What happened?" Cephas asks. "We did not say to stop."

Kitra and Achan notice us struggling to our feet.

"Explain," Kitra barks. "The rest of you people, be quiet!"

"I don't know," I say first. "But I've never had my power so drained." All true information. I really do not understand what happened, but it seems reasonable.

"Very well. This is a decent start. You may rest. You have earned it. Go to the dungeons. Stay in separate cells."

How thoughtful. We can lie down with the skeletons in piles of dirt and hay. I take one pained look at the chaos around me and fulfill my command.

22

AUGUST 30, 1866

I REACH OUT WITH MY SENSES AND FIND THE TWO NEW MAGICIANS CLOSING IN on a young woman. And after all, I've been asked to find her myself, so I see no reason not to bash both of the magician's heads into a tree trunk to prevent them doing so first. I may have been a tad rough with Pierce in particular, considering his nose is swollen to thrice its normal size, and his own blood is adding to the stain on his shirt.

Oh well. Such a shame.

I clean myself quickly and pop in the path of the fleeing girl. "Stop," I say, holding out a hand to her face.

"Where'd you come from?" she asks.

"You didn't see what you think you saw."

"I didn't see nothin'!" she shouts, backing away.

I recognize her now. She's one of the young servants from the plantation. And she's shaking so hard, I'm afraid she might shatter.

"It's okay," I say, raising my palms outward in surrender. Behind her, Caldor slips out of the shadows, shock and pain written plainly on his face.

"You aren't wearing a shirt," the woman says, distracting me.

Observant. "No. I'm not."

"You're Miss Lottie's friend."

Well, that title is debatable. "Yes. That's right."

She begins shaking her head back and forth, stumbling away from me. "You were one of them, weren't you? Were you? Did you?"

I sense a scream coming on, and I try to head it off. "No. No. I saw it too, though."

She doesn't trust me. Smart girl. But I need her to.

"What did you see?" she asks.

"I saw some men having a row."

"No. That weren't no row! That was a daemon from the depths of hell!" She crosses herself.

"What would make you say that?" I ask, keeping her focused on me as Caldor waits near the base of an enormous oak, hugging himself. A wolf howls in the distance. *Not helpful.*

"I need to get out of these woods. These are cursed woods, these are." Her voice is suddenly quiet and raspy.

"I will walk with you. I will protect you."

"What if you're one of them?" She looks about ready to bolt.

"If I were a daemon from hell, would I bother talking to you? Or would I kill you?"

"Just, just…" She strokes her throat. "Don't take my blood."

So she did see. Blast the full moon.

"Take your blood?" I ask, aghast, though my eyes are really on Caldor. The moonlight reflects off the moisture flowing down his cheeks, all I need to see to understand he's witnessed too much.

"I saw them," she says, sobs now breaking through so that my attention returns to my task. "Vampyres. That's what they was. They drink human blood in the night. Under the full moon."

"Ah. I see. Vampyres, you say?"

"Yes."

I have no doubt the original myth came from our own story. Kitra, Achan, Cephas. Yes, they were vampyres. Daemons from hell. Closer to it than I am, anyway. I reach for the servant's hand, but she still shrugs away.

"Prove you are not one of them," she says.

Like I'd try if I were. I think for a moment, sifting through memories for *what I know of the myths. Ah. I pull a small silver cross from inside my pants pocket, letting it glimmer in the moonlight. She relaxes at once.*

"Oh. Oh. I'm so sorry, Mister—"

"Taj," I say. "No need to be sorry after the fright you've had. Come and I will take you back up to the house."

"You didn't see?" she asks as I escort her to the gate. "Teeth like a lion, long and pointed. That's how they draw the blood."

I let her continue on about the things she believes she saw. There will be no further intervention necessary tonight. I watch her walk back toward the house, feeling his presence behind me.

"Why are you following me?" I ask without turning around. "If you have another command, I'd appreciate it if you just ask me straight out. It's been a rough night."

"I have no command. My master is asleep, and Mistress Lottie is otherwise occupied." Caldor's voice is filled with a warmth I have not before heard from him. When he sets his hand on my shoulder, it is like a butterfly's touch.

I turn to find him, face still wet with tears, inches from me. My insides burn with embarrassment. He knows what happened tonight—that is clear. It was not something I would have liked so many to witness.

"I am in need of rest." I sound tired. I am tired. Tired of living a life that does not belong to me.

To my surprise, Caldor lifts his hand from my shoulder and brushes away a tear I wasn't aware I'd shed. I freeze as he leans toward me, so slowly I wonder if time has stilled. His forehead touches mine, and his eyes close, brow furrowed with lines of pain and regret. His mouth is so close to mine that when he speaks, his warm breath tingles against my lips, tasting of coffee and apples.

"I am so sorry."

"Why?" I whisper, afraid he will move away and this one comfort will disappear.

"What happened to you...it was my fault for following a command I could not stop, yet I was angry at you for the exact same reason. I cannot have it both ways. But the thing is..." His eyes open, and the glistening shades of emerald and forest green swirl in a breathtaking dance before me. "I am glad for your company, Taj. I was frightened to admit it. I was scared you'd also be taken away. But you were right about taking what we can. And now I want whatever time I can steal."

My heart squeezes in my chest. It's true that he may be lying, though I cannot fathom what purpose it would serve. But I, too, crave the comfort of another of my kind.

When I don't move, Caldor does. He brushes his lips against mine, sending my nerve endings into overdrive. I open my mouth in invitation, and he slips his tongue inside, gently caressing my own in a dance that lights up my entire body. I lean into the kiss, into him for support because I am light-headed— whether from blood loss or whatever this is, I do not know. But strong arms pull me close, trailing over my back as our mouths move more fervently together, unable to get enough of each other.

He transports us to his modest room, and I am vaguely aware of the small bed beneath me and his skin hot against my own. I'm not really sure which of us removed our clothing, but it doesn't matter. He feels like heaven sliding against me, our erections rubbing together as we continue to explore each other's mouths and bodies. His nimble fingers trace the curves of my muscles, lighting a fire along their path. I reach down for his cock and stroke him slowly, drawing a deep moan from inside him that brings a smile to my face even as we kiss.

Caldor kisses his way down my body to my cock. He pauses, mouth open, and I strain not to shove it in his mouth. But he watches my face as he darts his tongue out to circle the tip. The intimacy of that gesture sends ripples of plea- sure that penetrate both my heart and body. I arch backward and groan with desire, needing more, needing him in every way.

He takes me inside, moving his mouth down over my shaft, deep into his throat, and pulls back slowly, letting his teeth lightly graze the sensitive skin until I'm literally begging him to continue. Being inside him, connected to him, is all I can think about. Thankfully, he complies, traveling up and down over me while I thrust my hips. As the overwhelming sensations consume me, I cannot hold back long. When my cock throbs with its release, Caldor pulls back slowly once again, sucking every last drop of orgasm from my body until I'm left a shuddering mess.

"Holy shit, that was amazing," I breathe.

"Glad I could make your night a little better." Caldor slides up my body and *lies against me, his own cock pressed against my thigh as he pulls me into his arms.*

In answer, I turn into his embrace and kiss him with abandon as I slide my hand down to bring him the same pleasurable release he's gifted me.

"You didn't kill them?" Charlotte screams at me from the doorway to her room.

She's back in her frilly gowns and trussed-up hair. I am in my gentleman's suit. You'd never know I was savaged under the moon in the woods a mere two hours ago. Or that I'd had a secret tryst in Caldor's room since.

"I followed your commands exactly," I say. "And you should be grateful."

Her face turns bright pink as she stalks forward. "So I see you haven't learned a damned thing from tonight." She slaps me.

"Master, if people in your mother's company begin to disappear, there will be great suspicion cast on your house, and you will lose some of your freedom. You have heard of the Salem Witch Trials, have you not?"

She steps back, uncertain.

"And as for lessons learned, if you, a mere child, did not glean anything from mine, what makes you think I—an eight-hundred-year-old Djinni—would suddenly change because of one night with you? Do you really imagine that you've shown me the worst of what a magician can offer? If only that were true." I allow a bitter laugh to escape my chest and fold my legs beneath me to float in the air.

I won't let her know that tonight may well have been one of the worst nights of my life until Caldor. Instead, thanks to him, I will show her that now that she's done her worst, I am still the same Djinni I was when she met me.

"I've adjusted Charles's memories," I say. "And as for the spy, she believes she saw monsters attacking someone. No more."

"You will sleep in the gazebo from now on," she says quietly. She turns her back to me, busying herself with the cushions on her bed. But I saw the tear trailing down her cheek. And I hear her sniff.

"Very well, Master. You will have to come fetch me then if you need anything."

I vanish, appearing outside the dreaded meadow. I know it is foolish of me, *but I fear the others will return to drink more blood while I am so helpless. The lead-induced pain I can stand. I've done it before, and it isn't pleasant, but I will survive.*

Perhaps if I do not "sleep" at all? I turn Charlotte's words around in my head. No good. I will sleep. I will sleep in the gazebo every night. And since there are only a few hours of "night" left, I find myself moving toward the old wooden steps and wondering for the millionth time in my life where Lee and Mira are right now.

23

REPRIEVE

WE AVOID THE LEAD-LINED CELL BUT REALIZE THE MOMENT WE STEP INSIDE, that there are enough trace amounts of the vile stuff added to each small room that we will remain weak until called for. More of Kitra's insurance, I suppose.

I settle down on the ground, as close to the door as possible, and tuck my knees up to my chin. My skin prickles from the lead, my head still pounds, and for whatever reason, my chest aches now as well. I open my mouth to speak, but my throat feels thick. I force through it anyway. This is our only chance for privacy other than while we are destroying the world.

"We have to find a way out." I sound rather hoarse.

Silence.

I fidget against the floor, scuffling the dirt and hay with my slippered feet.

"We cannot." Mira finally answers, in her usual bitter voice. The sound echoes off the walls, making it feel so final. So much stronger than my own.

I clear my throat and try again. "We will. This is not over. Far from it, Mir."

"And what would you have us do? We're all bound—not to one, but to three magicians. They now control every magician on this planet."

"I don't think we got them all," I say.

Silence.

"Something happened with the connection. Between Lee and me. We stopped it somehow."

"That's impossible." Mira again.

I think I hear Brolach whimpering somewhere to my left.

"Nor does it matter. The room was filled. There are four of us. Three of them."

"Lee—" I am about to tell Mira about what happened, but she doesn't let me.

"Lee is as good as dead," Mira spits.

I cringe, knowing Lee can hear every word but not respond.

"She cannot speak. She cannot move without permission. I'm surprised she can even breathe. It's over, Taj. Accept our fate. Kitra's right —this is what we were meant for."

My breath comes fast and hot, beating my chest from the inside. A single burning tear escapes and flows down my cheek. It doesn't matter. No one can see. Suddenly, I want to hurt Mira. Even more than I wanted to kill Kitra earlier.

"Brolach," I call. This time my voice is just as strong as Mira's, sounding back along the metal built into the corridor.

"Yes?" His voice is tentative but clear.

"I believe she will not watch you as carefully as the rest of us. She knows us. You have to look for any opportunities. Do you understand me?"

"Yes, Taj."

"You have to get out and get other Djinn to help. Tell them…tell them that if they don't, we will soon be coming for them all. It is the only way they can prevent enslavement."

"We could close the veil between worlds." The words hang in the space between us like poison.

He's right.

If we get that message through, we'd be trapped. But they'd stay free.

"Just look for a way out to warn them."

I lie down on my side, knees still curled up. I know there is an answer. I just have to find it. Have to save Lee. Even that ingrate Mira. This is my fault. My fault. My fault.

I wake to the sensation of being pulled through space and am deposited at Kitra's feet in her chambers. Perhaps the throne room is now too overcrowded with slaves. I focus on her face, so I do not have to search my memory for Sophie's. Or Jered's.

"You called, Master." I stand, suddenly aware that none of the others are there. I shift slightly on my feet.

"Taj. You are the leader, aren't you?"

I turn her words over in my mind. *Leader?* That is a human concept. "I don't think so," I say.

"Oh, I think you are. I see how you care for the others. You move first. You do what is hard and what must be done. Sometimes those things are one and the same, are they not?"

"I suppose."

"You speak for them too."

"Some of them cannot speak for themselves." I do not drop my gaze, though I fully expect retribution for speaking my mind.

"I see." She laughs and sits on the bed, patting the spot next to her.

I remain standing. She can command it if she wants to.

"Is there something you desire from me, Master?" Exhaustion settles deep in my bones. Not the kind that makes a human sleep, but the kind that comes from immortality when so many years are spent in trivial pursuits.

"As a matter of fact, there are many things I desire from you, Taj. The first is to make sure you are on my side."

"I have no choice but to be on your side, Master."

"True enough. But I desire more than obligation. Tell me, Taj, what do you think of Cephas?"

"He is a monster in a man's skin. And he is as dumb as a rock."

She laughs again. "Excellent. And what of Achan?"

"He is a coward. He disgusts me."

"Hmm. And the other Djinn?"

"They are my family. Lee and Mir. Brolach is not. He is…" I search for the word. "Delicate."

"So you feel protective of them?"

"Yes."

"And what do you think of me?" she asks, leaning forward in a rather seductive pose. How many centuries has she known me? Hasn't she figured it out yet?

"I think you are a manipulative, conniving bitch."

"You say that as though it's a bad thing."

"I also think," I continue, "that you've forgotten what it feels like to be human. That your soul is damned to hell. That you deserve to be tortured for the next five millennia for your crimes—"

"That will be enough." She sits straighter now, watching me. "I think we can come to some sort of agreement, Taj. You are certainly the most reasonable of your friends. As I say, you know what needs to be done."

"I cannot imagine, dear Master, what you could possibly think you must coax from me, when you have control over everything I do."

"I simply want to be sure. You can understand that, can you not?"

"Perhaps."

"Taj, I have the power to give you freedom of a sort. Room to breathe. To move. To do what you like."

"I am familiar with the definition." I cannot help but use sarcasm as a weapon, wishing she would get to the point and being unable to strike.

"No more witty retorts tonight, Taj." My mouth snaps shut. "Let me be plain. I am offering you the closest thing you will ever have to a normal life in exchange for your pledge that you will back me up if I need you to. And that you will help me—and you will tell no one this—find a way to kill Achan."

I do a pretty good job of not reacting. Perhaps my breathing speeds up ever so lightly, but all in all, I'm proud of myself.

"And the others?" If she feels she must barter, now is my chance.

"I do not trust Leela. I never will."

"I see. And do you trust Mira?"

"Mira is sensible, I think. I will not have to do what I've done with Leela."

"And Brolach?" I ask.

"Tell me, Taj, do you fancy him?" So she did notice.

"Anything I want from Brolach will come naturally and without force."

"Very well. I do not know him, but he is a Djinni, and I will be keeping an eye on him."

I nod. She takes that as agreement.

"You will let me know if you find any opportunities then," she says.

"I will kill him myself if you release your restrictive commands on Leela."

"You will do it anyway."

We stare at each other for a while. She cannot technically command this when he is also my master. Nor can I fulfill such a threat. So I'm not sure what she's up to. But I decide it isn't worth the potential misery to press her further.

"I will do as you command, Master."

"Good. Find yourself a room of your own. But, Taj?"

"Yes, Master?"

She rises, pulls me down to her, and presses her lips to my ear.

"Remember, I can make you very, very miserable in so many ways if I am displeased. Yes?"

Oh, don't I know it.

24

WISHES

KITRA'S VERSION OF FREEDOM INCLUDES ME AND MIRA BEING ABLE TO MOVE about the castle as we did over a year ago. Much of the free space is now taken by miserable-looking people. Slaves.

We must have gathered several hundred people before we fell. People of all races, all ages, all walks of life. People from all over the globe. Most look lost and confused. Once in a while, I find one that wears an expression of devastated understanding when he or she meets my eyes. Those are the ones who know what I am. What they are. Those are the ones I feel nothing for.

The Council, as Kitra has redubbed her group, has now gained three more Djinn through their little move. Those that their new slaves have been forced to turn over. Curiously, the others are kept away from us. I've heard only whispers in the crowded hallways, or I would never know at all.

Lee remains tethered to one of the Council at all times. I watch her despondent eyes as her gaze darts constantly around the room. Searching for one person I know she hopes did not make it here. She does not know that he was first taken by a murderer, that if he isn't here, he's dead. I wonder which she'd think is worse.

I've seen no sign of Sophie, making it more and more hopeful that we stopped before she was taken. I am daily grateful for that little miracle. I ignore the small piece of me that wishes I could take strength from a glimpse of her sweet face. I truly am a selfish ass.

I wish I hadn't fixed her memories after all. Now she'll know what and who is missing from her life. And why. I wonder if she'll be able to help Jered's mother cope with his disappearance.

I found Adia's last master fanning Kitra one day. When he saw my face, a malicious smile curled his lips. Glad to see that I, too, am suffering, I suppose. I left him to his job.

Now, I walk aimlessly down the corridors. Anything to avoid my masters and the others. Though I know it is an empty gesture because they can call me whenever they please. The only advantage of having so many others present is they have less of a need to do so.

I catch sight of Mira turning the corner ahead. Her eyes meet mine, and I almost look away. But she holds me somehow captive, finishing the distance calmly between us. Time slows. She brushes her hand against mine, slipping something inside my open palm.

Time resumes, and she continues down the hall and out of sight. I close my mouth and force myself forward around several more corners until I reach the kitchens. It is a place I normally avoid because the smells make me ill. As do the clanking of the pots.

Therefore it is perfect. My room is most likely under "observation." I lean into the corner, glance around for anyone who may be watching, and unfold the tiny piece of paper with trembling hands.

Tonight, after Council service. Dungeons.

The note dissolves in smoke as soon as I read it, and I peer around again to make sure no one is watching. What I see is the flash of a face disappearing through the rear doors.

Jered?

I run, bursting through into the hall outside the dining room. I search frantically in one direction and then the other, but I do not see him. Was he really there? Or was it because I'd been thinking about him? I bury my head in my hands and exhale deeply.

"Taj?"

My fingers crawl down my face of their own accord and reach out to stroke her small face. She leans into my hand, contentment written on her beautiful features. Her soft skin rubs my palm, her fine hair tickling my wrist.

She's real.

"Sophie." The one word is almost painful to utter. Because it makes it true. Seals her fate. "No."

I drop to my knees, and she throws her arms around my neck, hugging me tight. Slowly, I embrace her, rocking her back and forth, pressing my face into her strawberry-scented hair.

"Taj, I knew you'd find me."

How I wish I hadn't. But it feels so good to hear her voice. So normal.

"When can we go?" She looks so full of hope. So innocent.

"I...I..." *Can't finish the sentence.*

She pulls back, slipping her fingers against the velvet ribbon around my neck. I squeeze my eyes shut because I cannot bear to see her face fall.

"It's okay, Taj."

I open my eyes. She still looks full of hope.

"Everything will be okay," she says.

Shouldn't I be the one saying this?

"I love you. You'll protect me. I know it."

I stand, backing into the wall. Away from her. My throat closes, and my chest tightens. Tears burn behind my eyes, and I shake uncontrollably. I dig my fingernails into the rock until blood oozes warm and fresh over my hands. Some sort of wheezing sound escapes my mouth. She's asking the impossible. Doesn't she see I'm dangerous? They could make me hurt her. Everyone I've ever dared to love has been hurt by my own hand, and there is nothing I can do to stop it. If I harm Sophie, it will break me.

"Taj?" She puts a small hand on my vest, tugging.

"You have to stay away from me, Sophie. Do you understand? I am dangerous. I am not safe. I will hurt you." *Keep it together.*

"No. You wouldn't."

I cry outright now, tears sliding onto her head. "It doesn't matter. I can't stop it, Sophie. You have to stay as far away from the others as you can. From Kitra, your father, Cephas. From us too."

She shakes her head back and forth, furrowing her brow, backing away from me. I can't stand any more. So I disappear. I go to my room. But when I appear, I am not alone. Kitra is waiting.

"You look upset, Taj."

I gather my outward appearance as learned from years of experience. "I've been viewing your subjects today. Misery is contagious." I collapse on the bed and turn my head to watch her.

"I see. I want you to give me an onyx."

"You already have one." I can say it because it is true, and she did not phrase it as a command. I smile. "Is the one tied to me not enough?"

Anger flashes in her eyes, but she regains her cool composure in seconds, returning my smile. She saunters to my spot on the bed and leans down, letting her dark hair fall around me.

"It is very precious to me. But the one you will make me is a fake that looks exactly like the one I have."

Not wishing to bring any more hardship upon myself, I raise my hand in front of her face, offering the stone she's asked for. She snatches it from me and stands.

"Anything else, Master?" I ask.

"You will watch my back. If you see any sign of trouble from either another Djinni or any magicians, you will put a stop to it immediately."

"Yes, Master."

"Good. Very good." She leaves.

An hour until the Council Service. I begin pulling onyxes from the air above me and crushing them to dust in my hand.

25

SEPTEMBER 22, 1866

CHARLOTTE HAS TAKEN TO HAVING VISITORS IN HER CHAMBERS LATE AT NIGHT. *Specifically Pierce or Lucas. Though she seems to favor Lucas the most, with his wavy strawberry-blond hair and strong square chin. I can't say I blame her. Both boys are quite attractive, but Pierce's eyes have not completely lost their madness since that night in the meadow.*

I fully expect her to pick Lucas for her betrothed, even before I find him waiting with her on her bed. She is already dressed in her nightgown, and I notice all the servants are scarce.

I hesitate at the door. "I will retire to the gazebo, then," I say. She need not know I plan to meet Caldor first as I have every night since she served my blood on a platter.

"No, wait!" Lucas says with a laugh.

I look at Charlotte. For he is not my master. "What is it, darling?" she asks.

"Lottie's told me what you did to her," he says, speaking directly to me instead. He rises and strides to meet me. I am tall, but he has a good three inches on me. Not that physical berth really matters.

"What I did to her?" I ask.

"How you nearly forced yourself on her."

Oh, that is rich. I laugh. And he looks murderous, so I shut up. "And did she tell you of the command she gave me?" I ask in my most innocent voice.

He does not take his eyes from mine, but a line appears on his forehead. Good. I wait. When he says no more, I turn to go. "You know where I'll be."

"Stop," *he says.* "I want to watch you suffer."

I turn and sigh. If I had a nickel for every time a magician said that...

He waves a hand through the air, and heavy lead cuffs appear in his hands. I take a step back, again looking at Lottie. I guess I don't really expect her to be helpful here.

"Taj, you will do what Lucas tells you." *She is absolutely delighted. Her face is flushed. Her gallant beau has come to rescue her from the big bad Djinni. Lovely.*

"Well, in that case, I don't believe I'll be needing these after all," *Lucas says, making them disappear.*

I freeze. I don't dare even breathe. This is it, the moment I've been expecting. I can feel it as surely as I could feel the presence of the lead moments ago. He wanted control. What I don't know is who will win this battle. And I will not choose sides prematurely.

"You would prefer to beat him with your very masculine hands?" *Charlotte asks, taking hold of his wrist and dotting the inside of it with a kiss.*

Lucas smiles. Can she see the hunger in his eyes? Or does she assume it is a different kind of hunger?

"Taj," *he says, gaze still on Charlotte.* "Take her voice."

Her face falls. She opens her mouth to scream, but it is already done. Her gaze darts to mine, filled with fear, and all I can do is shake my head piteously. I warned her. Despite everything, I tried.

"You will no longer obey her commands."

"You may not order that," *I say automatically.* "She is my master."

"How?" *he asks. Smart man. He could have easily begun beating me senseless for talking back. Instead he heard my words.*

"My stone," *I say, pulling down my collar for him to see.*

His eyes grow wide with understanding, and he pulls Charlotte over to him roughly, dipping his hand between her breasts to retrieve the amulet. She tries so hard to scream, her face turns purple. Still not a sound emerges as he tugs it off and clutches it in his hand.

"Now?" *he asks.*

"Yes." *It is done. Outwardly, I show no sign of panic. Inside, I scream because I do not know what this will mean for Caldor and me. I have not had a chance at happiness like this for many years, and it hurts to think I may have already lost it.*

26

COUNCIL SERVICE

THE THRONE ROOM IS EMPTIED OF ALL MAGICIANS SAVE THE COUNCIL. I stand hand in hand with Lee, Mira, and Brolach. We've done it every night since the first. An hour of time devoted to filling the various needs of our masters. They have determined that the optimum amount of time is one hour. After that, we become too drained to continue. I wonder why they have not added the other three to the mix.

We rarely speak to one another despite the seemingly golden opportunity. In fact, it has become an hour of pure hell. All Lee will do is whisper Jered's name over and over in her mind, so I have avoided reaching out to her for the past week. I can only take so much. Mira will answer my call, but continues to suggest I accept my fate. Brolach is far too nervous to be useful, though I do enjoy talking to him on better days. It is tempting to push further with him, but I've done so before, and it didn't end well. If he shows interest, I will respond, but emotionally it would be far better for me to make myself unavailable. No. I've decided to let the others be the ones to initiate contact.

So I am very surprised when Lee's essence flows over my own and whispers, *Are you okay?*

We are in the midst of tampering with the minds of several American congressmen so that things will move in the Council's favor. Kitra decided that it would be better to rule the world in a less visible way. Less irate peasants to deal with apparently.

Lee? It's the only answer I have.

I'm sorry, she says. I have no words. *I abandoned you when you needed me. Old habits die hard I suppose. It's just that I thought I had more time… I.* She pauses, *I thought I'd have one lifetime with him. I always knew it would end but I thought I deserved. I thought maybe.*

I know the pain she feels. Love so new, stolen from your grasp is not an easy thing to deal with. *Lee, you do deserve it. You deserve more than one lifetime of happiness. Jered, he loved you. Loves you.*

I see a tear slide down her cheek to my right. But her face remains impassive.

He's a good man, Lee. A strong man. He's never been afraid to stand up to me when I act like an asshole.

You mean, weekdays? she asks.

Yes. I squeeze her hand.

I wonder why he never came. Even in my mind, the thought feels like a whisper, and I know it costs her to admit it. To admit that she wanted him to try. I remember how much I wished to see Sophie's face. Then I recall the reality of seeing her there.

Lee gasps. *You saw Sophie? Oh, no. She cannot be here, Taj!*

You heard that, eh? I know. I know, Lee. She's okay. I told her to keep away.

Taj, you have to do something.

Well, that irks me. Why should I be the one who must do something? *Don't you think I want to?*

I can't. They've seen to that. I have nothing. You have the most freedom of all of us. You will find a way. Lee is as vehement as I am.

I flash back to Kitra's words. *You are the leader, aren't you?* Funny, I don't remember running for the position.

But it's true, Taj. You've always been the glue that holds us together. The strong one. I trust you, Taj. I promise I will do all I can if you promise me the same.

"Very good. I believe I am done for this evening. Achan?" Kitra asks.

"Done," he says, looking longingly at Lee.

"Cephas?" Kitra asks.

"I have someone waiting for me in my chambers."

Of course you do.

"Very well, you are dismissed. Leela, you will accompany Cephas this evening."

Cephas looks as though he means to say something and then thinks better of it. I can almost see the lightbulb go on over his head. Leela drops my hand and walks to his side, where she kneels obediently. I feel my eyes glow.

"Actually," Achan says, "I was thinking I would enjoy Leela's company this evening."

Kitra's smile is forced. "I was hoping to have a private audience with you." She runs her fingers along his arm.

Achan is clearly surprised by this. Then I know. She had me create the fake so she could switch it with his and have me kill him. *Do it*, I will him. I want nothing more than to fulfill that one command.

He's torn. I can see it in the way his fist clenches at his side. His gaze darting from one woman to the other—a triangle over a thousand years in the making. Though in this case, neither woman really wants him, yet he has his choice of both.

"Why not bring her with us?" he says finally, flashing his dazzling smile at Kitra. "I know how you like to keep an eye on her."

"You afraid of me mistreating your little whore?" Cephas asks.

Lee remains head down, still, as they debate her fate. Bile rises in my throat, and I feel my mouth twist into a sneer. Kitra's gaze passes over me, and I quickly adjust. But she's seen, and if I'm not mistaken, she nods almost imperceptibly in my direction.

"Now boys, do not fight over the tart. There are so many to choose from."

To my left, Mira stiffens. If they take her, she will not be able to meet me in the dungeons. But how can I stop it? How can I stop any of it?

"Cephas, you already have company. Go enjoy yourself. I promise her to you tomorrow. We can bring her along tonight if you like, Achan. I'm sure she will make herself useful in some capacity." Kitra's eyes rest again on mine, but this time I am stone.

Cephas leaves, and Mira relaxes. Achan waits for Kitra to move first.

"You go ahead. I will be up in a moment," she purrs.

Achan strides from the room. Lee follows in his wake like a shadow. Kitra descends from her dais, runs a hand over Brolach's shoulder, and whispers in his ear, loud enough for us to hear. "Tomorrow night is all for you."

"Yes, Master," he says, trembling even more than usual.

Kitra kisses his cheek and sweeps from the room while Brolach ducks out behind her, unable to meet our eyes. My stomach turns. He's but a babe in human skin. Was Kitra his introduction to so-called pleasure of the flesh? Is this another thing to add to my guilty conscience?

27

IN THE DUNGEON

MIRA RAISES HER EYEBROWS AND DISAPPEARS WITH A FLOURISH OF HER hands. I pace the floor for a few minutes more before joining her. But when I do appear in the bottom levels, I find more than just Mira waiting for me.

"Hello, Taj." Jered grins at me from where he leans against the wall, hands tucked casually in his jeans pockets. He looks especially handsome in his long-sleeve black Oxford shirt. A little too clean. A little too well. A little too alive.

So I really had seen him today. A hand flutters to my chest. "Dear God. Has Lee—"

"No! She can't know," Jered says, standing tall, striding forward to face me. "I don't want her to see that I am a slave, Taj. It would kill her. I can't do that."

"But—"

"Taj, Jered wants to help us." Mira tugs at my arm. "He's rounding up the human slaves. Preparing them for a rebellion."

"How?" I croak.

"We aren't Djinn, Taj. We are human. And those of us lucky enough not to have been bewitched before you stopped? We can fight."

"She'll just realize she missed a few of you and have us stifle that part into submission. Stamp it out," I say, conjuring a chair and sitting down before I faint between the surprise and stress of the situation.

"You are the one who continues to pester me!" Mira screams. "You are the one who cannot give up. I bring you Jered. Alive. And you tell him not to bother?"

She slaps me hard across the face, and I nearly fall out of my chair. I right myself to find Jered squatting before me, imploring with his big dark eyes.

"I will save her, Taj. With or without your help."

I want to say so much. That I've tried. That I can't believe he didn't reveal himself earlier. That Mira is right and we should give up. But what I do say is, "I'll do anything."

"Divide and conquer. That's the plan," Jered says.

"Where were you?" I ask him, as he paces the floor away from me.

"Here," he says, turning to look at me.

"No. Before. We came for you, to rescue you, and we found the other Djinn, but not you. You were gone, and then there was nothing. The alarms were never set off, no more Djinn have died. But I thought—"

"You thought I was dead."

"Yes."

"I was close. Then I was here. And I somehow knew I was brought here to serve. Of course I knew right away who, and why. It isn't my first visit. Been sure to steer clear of dear ol' Dad though."

He sounds too casual. Too self-assured. Surely inside he's crying like a baby. I look at Mira. Perhaps he is putting on a front for us, so we will agree to his plan.

"Have you seen her?" I ask.

"We don't have time for this," Mira says, exasperated. "We have so little opportunity to talk."

"I'm going to kill Achan," I blurt out. I cannot discuss Kitra's plan. But I fully intend to fulfill this promise.

"One of us will. Certainly," Jered says.

Something is not right. But I am far too tired and confused to understand. Does he know about Sophie?

"Sophie is here." I watch him carefully for a response.

He swallows, a shadow passing over his features. His gaze flits over Mira and then me. "Oh my God." I conjure another chair just in time, as he drops from his feet.

"She needs to lie low," he says, pinching the bridge of his nose.

"I told her. I'm not sure she understands, though." *She thinks I can protect her. You all seem to for some reason, even though I'm the reason we're here.*

Jered nods, as though having some internal dialogue with himself. Then he looks at me with such intensity, I shift my gaze to Mira.

"Now what?" I ask. He can be the leader for a change.

"We take them out, one by one," he says. "Can you get Cephas alone in his room tomorrow?"

I recall Kitra's promise that he will have Lee tomorrow. "Tonight," I say. "I know he's got only one other with him tonight. He'll probably drink himself to sleep. I remember his habits well."

"Fine. You make sure he's alone in two hours, and I will kill him." Did *Jered* just say that? I guess a little indentured servitude can really change a man.

"As soon as she finds the body, she'll put this whole place on lockdown," I say. "You need to take out Achan first."

"What? Why will that help?" Mira asks.

"Just trust me. You asked for my input by bringing me here."

Jered interrupts whatever retort Mira had in store for me. "I will kill Cephas tonight. Achan in the morning before he is discovered. Can you get him alone, Mira?"

"I believe so. If Kitra has left his chambers."

"Fine. I'll wait until I see her leave, and then I will make my move. Once we've got it down to just her, things will be much easier."

"Jered, no!" Sophie jumps out of the shadows near the stairs and runs to her brother.

Jered's face falls for a moment, and then he's as cool as before, squatting down to accept his sister's embrace.

"Sophie, what are you doing here?"

"Jered, you can't do it. You can't just kill people like that."

"Sophie, you don't understand. It's the only way to make this end. It's how to save Leela. They're evil, Soph. No question, no doubt. Just evil."

Sophie's face is stained with tears. Her tiny shoulders shake through her sobs. "No. You can't. You're not like them."

"Sophie, you're too young for this. You shouldn't be here." Jered's face turns crimson, and he stands, pulling away from her. "You need to go. To stay away from us until this is over. I thought you explained this, Taj."

"Don't blame him! He didn't know I followed him. I...I couldn't let you leave me. I don't know where to go. Mommy isn't here. I couldn't find you, Jered."

Jered turns away, unable to face her, so I scoop her into my arms and cradle her trembling body until she quiets down.

"We want to protect you, Sophie," I say in the soft voice I couldn't manage earlier. "But we cannot do that until we take care of the Council."

She sniffles, looks up at me with those huge blue eyes, and seems to steel herself like a much older person. "I want to help then."

"You can't. You're too young—" Jered starts.

"Yes," I say, cutting him off. "You can. Here's what I want you to do."

We review our plans. Sophie kisses my cheek and races up the stairs. Jered leaves with one icy glare in my direction. The silence between Mira and me is awkward at best.

"I'm sorry I tried to convince you to give up, Taj."

"Mir, did you tell Jered about the three stones?" I ask suddenly.

"No."

"Then how did he know all three of them had to be taken out?"

Mira looks uncomfortable and surprised, both unusual enough on their own.

"He's just going on the information he had from before. He knows how they work," she reasons. It sounds more like she's trying to convince herself than me.

"I should go," I say, rising. "Thank you, Mir. You always come through when I need you."

"You mean despite my tendency to be a pain in the ass?"

28

SEPTEMBER 22, 1866

Lucas throws Charlotte to the bed. "Tie her down. I can't have the others in the house learning anything. They don't even know I come here."

I snap, and she is bound to the bedposts, still struggling. But her power is nothing compared to mine. I'm not sure if she really ever understood that until this moment.

Master Lucas begins to pace. I watch as my heart races, unwilling to relax. This could still play out against him. Does he know of the Widow Wilde and Caldor? How much has this foolish child shared with him?

He stops and speaks directly to Charlotte. "I do care for you, Lottie. I hate seeing you like this."

She spits at him.

"I've done this for your own good, you know. I still want you to be my wife. If you will act like nothing is wrong, be the perfect Southern gentlewoman, you will have complete run of the house, all the servants you could ask for. Anything you desire."

She spits again.

"It is either that or an unfortunate accident."

She stills, her chest pumping in and out with each heavy breath. Finally she nods.

"Taj," he says, facing me. "Can you guarantee her compliance?"

"I do not have that kind of power, Master Lucas. However," I say, and see her eyes widen with fear. "I can alter her memories. I can take away certain words. What I cannot change is her will. Her emotions."

He chews on this information, again having taken it in as opposed to lashing out against it. If he hadn't pulled my blood from my neck, I might have an ounce of respect for him.

"Can you make it so that she can only speak in my company? And that she cannot leave these rooms unless I allow it?"

"It is within my ability." I take in her now pale face. The Buddhists believe in the concept of Karma. Western religions—an eye for an eye. Perhaps I have grown too soft, but as the victim, I take no pleasure in this kind of torment. Still, it means I am able to remain on the plantation. Remain near Caldor.

"Do it. Then let her up."

I clap my hands, making Charlotte wince. But when she opens her eyes, her hands are free. She touches her lips. She is in his company. She should be able to speak.

"I told you I will agree to your demands," she says, trembling.

"Lottie, darling, I love you. But I do not trust you. Now if you will excuse us, Taj? I believe we have an engagement announcement to plan. And some celebrating to do."

I leave. I do not wish to witness that anyway.

At least I do not have to sleep in the gazebo tonight. That is the information I lead with when I inform Caldor of what happened. But when I move to stroke his arm, he stiffens beneath my touch.

"Have I said something wrong?" I slide closer to him and nuzzle his ear.

"You could have been taken from me just like that. It could have happened so fast I'd never even know where you went. I may never have seen you again."

I reach for his face and turn him to look at me. "That is the nature of our predicament. But why waste time with worry about what is inevitable when we can make each moment together last?" I dive in for a kiss before he can respond.

He pushes against my chest with his palms, and reluctantly I back up.

"Perhaps you are used to this, having had so many masters, and perhaps as many lovers. This is relatively still new to me, Taj. I want...I want to find a way for us to be together permanently. I...I think I love you."

My pulse pounds with the sound of the words. True, I've had many lovers, but this is the first time that particular feeling has been mutual. "Then we will do our best to be devious Djinn." I pull him to me and make love with abandon, knowing not just his body, but his heart belongs to me as well.

29

THE BEST LAID PLAN

CEPHAS'S DOOR IS AJAR WHEN I ARRIVE AT THE APPOINTED TIME. IT ISN'T difficult to see why. Cephas is sound asleep, judging by the snoring, and the poor female is trying so hard to step through the threshold that there are claw marks etched in the stone, her hands covered in a mixture of dried and fresh blood. Upon seeing me, she cringes back to the floor, arms raised above her head.

I kneel beside her, gently prying her hands away from her face. She is a pretty girl. About Jered's age, with wild, light-brown hair and hazel eyes clouded with tears. I hush her softly and concentrate, healing her fingers and bruises. She blinks.

"There is a spell on the door preventing you from passing through," I say, brushing her hair from her face.

She looks mortified. I smile.

"So we'll just send you through the wall."

I take her hand, help her to her feet, and step with her through the stone and metal, seeing her safely to the other side. She stares around for a moment, opens her mouth, then shuts it again, and runs.

Good luck hiding.

I wait outside the door, casually leaning against the wall until Jered shows. He's dressed all in black. Turtleneck, pants, and shoes. I snicker at him, though I suppose it's a valiant attempt at camouflage.

"He's alone?" Jered asks.

"Still angry, huh? Oh well, I suppose you can use that when you're murdering the jolly green giant in there."

He stares, nostrils flared, fists clenched.

"Yes. He's alone." I stand up straight. "And out cold."

Jered nods, takes a deep breath, and steps through the threshold. I go invisible and follow. I'm not sure what use I can be since I cannot technically betray Cephas, but I might think of something if the situation calls for it.

Jered approaches slowly, though it isn't necessary. I doubt World War III would wake Cephas right now. Ah, the memories. He makes it to Cephas's side, and looks down, disgusted, at his sleeping form.

Jered covers his mouth and nose, probably to protect himself from the stench. Cephas still never asked us to fix his rotted teeth. And of course no one's offered. Jered turns away to collect himself and then back, pulling a long, thin rapier from the air before him. The glint of silver in the moonlight flashes across his eyes, and for the first time, I see Achan in him.

I tense as Jered points the tip of the sword to Cephas's heart. The giant's eyes snap open, blind with sleep and the sudden threat. Jered's hand jerks at the sight of him, his breath speeding up, and he thrusts the tip through Cephas's chest with all his strength.

Time slows. My eyes open wide right along with Cephas's. A horrible gurgling sounds from his chest, and a trail of blood trickles from the corner of his mouth. His hands twitch upward, grabbing for Jered's sleeves, but Jered twists the sword again. The huge outstretched hands stop in their tracks and fall to his side. His eyes roll up in his head, and both Jered and I let out a breath. We are both shaking.

"Give me the stones." I materialize at his side.

Jered stares blankly at me and swallows, still clutching the sword hilt stuck through Cephas's chest.

"He's dead," he says.

"Generally that's what happens when you stab someone through the heart. Now give me the stones. I don't want them lying around."

Jered nods slowly, finally releasing the weapon. He takes one look at what he's done and vomits all over the floor.

So I pull the sword out of his chest, making the body jerk involuntarily, and yank back the covers. My gaze trails down his body, searching out my quarry. They are there, lying askew on the pillow, still tied to his neck by a black cord. Four stones. Onyx, diamond, emerald, and moonstone.

I reach for them but cannot grasp them. What is this? I start to panic, watching the hole in Cephas's chest as it ever so slowly begins to close. Shit.

"Jered! Take them. NOW."

Jered hesitates, yellow in the pale light of the room. He seems upset, but sees my face and yanks the necklace off Cephas's neck. I breathe again and pop us both out of the room and into the dungeon.

"What the hell?" Jered asks, looking around.

"He isn't dead. You didn't kill him."

"I stabbed him through the heart. You saw it, Taj."

"I couldn't touch the stones. I saw the wound healing."

"How is that possible?" Is that relief I hear in Jered's voice?

"We granted them immortality in their original bodies. I guess we went all out. I thought they could still die of unnatural causes. But four Djinn together..."

"Shit. He saw me, Taj!" Jered paces, running a hand through his sandy hair.

"Give me the necklace. I can alter his memories. He is no longer my master."

Jered stops and meets my gaze as my hand remains outstretched and empty. He swallows, and I cannot discern what he's feeling. Conflicted?

"Give me the goddamn necklace, Jered."

"I can't."

"What?"

"I'm your master."

"*What?*"

"Taj, I...I can't. If I'm in control too, we can fight Kitra's influence. Think about that."

My eyes burn, and the muscles in my neck twang. *Calm down, Taj. Calm down.* Maybe he's right. Maybe this is better. I still belong to the others. We all do. With him also in control, we can manipulate—even contradict—some of their commands. They don't know that he is not under their control. I'm not even sure they know he's here.

"Command me to fix his memory, keep him in the room for the day, and give him fakes," I say in answer, closing my outstretched hand into a fist.

"Do it."

30

FACE-TO-FACE

"This changes things." Jered continues to pace. "I can call Leela to me." He strokes the diamond tenderly.

"No, you cannot," I say. "She's with them. They'll know something is wrong."

"She's with them?" His voice breaks on the last word. He wears his pain like a badge of honor, this kid.

"I didn't want to tell you, but we can't blow your cover. I'm sorry."

He slides to the ground, clutching the necklace, and then pulls it over his head, tucking it beneath the turtleneck.

"Master?" I ask. He winces like I drove a sword through his heart. "How did you know that they all have stones?"

Fear. That's what I see in his eyes this time, and I shift uncomfortably in my chair. Again there is a nagging feeling that I am missing something important.

"Who does the fourth stone belong to?" Jered asks.

"Brolach. The Djinni who tried to kill you in my bedroom. What happened after you were taken?"

"I have to go."

"Where—"

"Stop!" He screams, and it echoes along the walls.

My lips clamp shut.

His chest moves rapidly up and down beneath his shirt. "I'm sorry."

He takes the stairs three at a time as he runs away. Somehow, I don't think he's going to be able to outrun whatever this is, though.

I pop upstairs to find the first rays of morning light fighting their way through the haze of dust and gloom making up the fortress. If Jered thinks I'm going to be a good little Djinni and wait around to see what happens with Achan, well, he's certifiable.

I head straight for Achan's rooms. The moment I turn the corner toward his chambers, I nearly crash into Brolach. My gaze trails longingly down his bare chest, peeking through his vest, and then back up to his face.

"Oh, Taj! I'm so glad it's you." He embraces me at once, his breath coming hot against my neck. He smells like clover, though how I do not know.

I return his embrace and then gently pull him away so that I can talk to him.

"What is it, Brolach?"

"I felt something. And I don't know, but I think something's happened with the Council. Hopefully something bad," he adds in a hushed voice.

"Yes, well, you could say that." I allow myself to laugh a little. "Cephas has lost his stones to Jered. But he doesn't know they're gone."

Shock. Then, "Jered? You mean Leela's boyfriend? The one I almost killed?" His voice gets higher with each word.

"The one and only. But don't worry, I'm sure he wouldn't hold a grudge. Now you go make your pretty little self scarce, and hopefully by the end of the day, we'll be back home celebrating."

He blinks at me, flashes me his supermodel grin, and entwines his fingers with mine. Mira appears at the far end of the hall, then his lips are on mine, and I am distracted.

It's something I've been longing to do since I saw him here. Something I couldn't bring myself to admit I'd be willing to risk. I feel responsible for his situation. How can I ask him for what I don't deserve? What I can't protect us from?

But he's the one to make the move...his lips are so warm and firm. His tongue like heaven. I press him to me, running my hands through his silken hair, inhaling him. But moments later, I pull away, tilting his chin up to look me in the eyes.

"I have to go. But we'll pick up where we left off later."

He smiles again, looking far more relaxed than when I found him, and I let him go. He allows his fingers to trail down my arm and across my own hand, before taking off around the corner.

Mira waits for me before the double doors. She's staring at Kitra's symbol etched into the metal. The sun with the eye, the moon, and the star. She's somewhere far away.

I place a hand on her shoulder to get her attention and fill her in on what happened with Cephas. She frowns and tilts her head to the side, letting her hair spill over her shoulder.

"You have to get Lee out of there somehow. Before he sees her there. He has to be on top of his game, Mir. I'll take care of Kitra."

"If we can't kill them, how will we ever be rid of them?" she whispers.

"We'll cross that bridge when we come to it," I say. "Let's go."

Drawing a deep breath, I fling open the door and kneel.

"Taj?" Kitra asks.

She is wrapped in a crimson robe, seated on the edge of the bed. I hear the shower going in the other room and assume that is where Achan has gone. Lee sits in the corner, staring straight ahead. There are no visible signs of abuse, but I cannot think about it now. I must carry out the plan we made in the dungeon.

"Master, you are alone." I feign relief.

"Is something wrong?"

"Yes. You recall our conversation, Master?"

"Of course I do. Get to the point."

"I have found a way to carry out your...request. But you must go now. If it fails—" I look her directly in the eye.

"Very well. Come." She rises and beckons me to her, where she touches her mouth to my ear. "I have replaced the stone with the copy."

"Perfect, Master."

Kitra looks downright pleased with me. She touches my face and leaves. I glance at Lee, my chest heavy, and disappear.

Mira nearly bumps into Kitra on her way inside. Perfect.

"You clumsy little—"

"Forgive me, Master. I've been sent to collect Leela for Cephas as you promised. He asked me to hurry."

"I see. Well, get on with it then, and watch what you're doing."

"Yes, Master." Mira turns to Lee. "You will come with me."

Kitra leaves, but Lee does not move to obey. Damn. She doesn't have to. She doesn't follow Cephas's commands any longer. I thought she'd do it out of habit or assumption or something, but apparently, she's put herself on autopilot, letting her body behave as told without having to think about it. Not a bad way to cope, really.

"Lee." I lean down for her. "You have to go with Mir. You aren't going to Cephas." She focuses on me and stands, taking my hand.

She's about to follow Mira out when Jered enters the room. Their eyes meet, and everything stops. Unfortunately, so does the sound of the shower.

"You have to go. Now," I say to Mira, and even I can hear the desperation in my voice.

"Leela," Jered says, holding out a hand to her. Her mask crumbles to pieces, and she falls.

I am there in a flash, gathering her in my arms. Jered looks like he's been stabbed again. Shit.

Mira snaps. She and Lee disappear from the room as the door opens, and Achan comes out in the same kind of robe Kitra had. Very pretty. He sees me first and stops in his tracks, confused. By the time he turns to face Jered, his son has pulled another sword from the air and is aiming it at his chest. There is murder in Jered's dark eyes. So much hatred that he is shaking, his face twisted in a very unattractive way.

"Taj," Achan squeaks. "Kill him."

"Oh, no can do. So sorry. See, you are no longer my master. Funny thing, though, your son here? He *is*." I examine my nails while I wait for his reaction.

"Son, you cannot do this. I didn't know you were here. You can join me now. I don't need your body anymore."

"I'm sure my master here appreciates the thoughtfulness of your offer," I interject, seeing that Jered's in no mood to talk. "But I think he's also a tad upset about you kidnapping his girlfriend, taking her freedom, and nearly extinguishing her humanity."

Hearing me say it spurs something inside Jered, and he begins to shake harder with fury, like he's having his own personal earthquake. I'm surprised Achan hasn't already bought it. Not that he can actually die. Pity that.

"I don't have to kill him," Jered spits.

"What?" both Achan and I ask.

"Give me the stones. All of them."

Achan hastens to oblige. Nothing is more important than his pathetic life. He hands Jered four rings from his fingers, nearly impaling himself on the tip of the sword when Jered does not move it from its position, centered on Achan's heart.

"Now make him forget. Give him fakes. You can destroy these." Jered tosses me the rings, which I crush immediately.

"Thank you, son." Achan tries his winning smile.

"You deserve to die."

I fulfill my command, but before I do, I grab the sword from Jered's hand and run it through Achan's throat. He gurgles. Blood spurts like a fountain from the point of entry, coating my chest, and Jered's shocked face. I watch with pleasure as the bastard drops to his knees, eyes gone glassy. I pull the weapon out and hold it up as his body falls to the ground, twitching in a pool of his own blood.

"That's how you run someone through with a sword, kid," I say.

"I told you to make him forget."

"And so I will. Right away. But don't tell me you aren't glad I did it. Even if it won't stick."

Jered puts a hand to his forehead and squints in pain. I forgot about his little problem. He speaks through it as I replace the rings and wave away the mess along with Achan's memories.

"What's wrong with Leela?"

"She was just surprised to see you."

"Taj!"

"She'll be okay. As soon as we're done with Kitra." I clap a hand on his back, and he manages a brave smile. But it doesn't reach his eyes. I can't blame him.

I don't believe me either.

31

OCTOBER 18, 1866

I BELIEVE THE WIDOW WILDE IS BECOMING SUSPICIOUS. AND I DO NOT FULLY understand why Lucas allows Pierce to make himself at home on this plantation. Charlotte does a grand job pretending to be thrilled with her new fiancé, perhaps actually enjoying the attention of all her many admirers.

Such gatherings bore me terribly, and I decide to take a walk around the grounds to enjoy the cooler weather. I haven't gone far, however, when Pierce falls into step with me. I clench my fist at my other side, ready.

"I wanted Lottie," he says.

"How disappointing."

"Past tense. Wanted. Now I know what I really want is power."

One glance tells me his magician's aura is pulsing with vivid bursts of red, purple, and blue. The colors swirl and coalesce into an ever-changing mixture. Something about it is more tumultuous than the others. More chaotic. I keep my fist ready.

"It would seem," I say, since he waits for a response, "you have that now. You cannot garner more the same way, though. Sorry to disappoint."

"I am aware of the limitations," he says. "I have other plans, however."

Oh goody. Another grab for power. I feel like I'm being spun round blindfolded in a game of blindman's bluff.

"*Good for you. Now, if you will excuse me, I'd like to enjoy my moment of peace.*"

"*Of course. But know that it will happen. Tonight, in fact. And you will help me.*"

"*Oh. Do your new powers include prophetic visions?*" *I ask.*

Much to my delight, he moves to strike, sending a burly hand toward my face. Time slows, and I decide that just this once I will do it the human way. I catch his fist in my hand and squeeze. Tiny bones begin to crunch beneath the pressure, and his face goes white. I swing my other hand, already balled up, right into his cheek. Blue lightning crackles when I make contact, and he flies back onto the ground, blood spraying from his mouth.

All right, I guess it wasn't entirely the human way. But close enough. And quite, quite satisfying.

I brush my hands off on my pant legs and whistle, continuing my stroll toward the cotton fields, enjoying the sound of the birds and the scent of autumn, courtesy of the newly fruited apple trees. Ahh.

When I am far enough away from sight of the main house, Caldor appears beside me, taking my hand in his. I cannot keep the smile from blooming. I am about to tell him about my encounter when I recall the reaction he'd had when Lucas stole me from Lottie. I sneak a glance at his profile, bathed in the afternoon sun like a halo. His innocence is so beautiful, and how long can he hold on to it, realistically? I don't want to be the one to take that from him or to cause him to worry.

So I squeeze his hand and begin to whistle as we stroll.

32

REUNION

"You need to sleep, Master."

Jered cringes as I help him into my bed. "Please stop saying that."

"Fine. I won't tell you what you need. You're a big boy, figure it out yourself."

"No. I mean the 'Master' thing."

"So you command." I cringe at the horrified look on his face. "Sorry. Force of habit."

"Where did Mira take her?"

He won't let me touch his clothes but does allow me to slip off his shoes and pull the blankets over him. "She has to hold her because of the command, Jered."

"Hold her?" He sits up, and the blankets fall.

I gently push him back and start tucking again. "She's supposed to always be by one of them. Her command unless we prevent it."

"Oh, God. Taj. I need to go." He throws my work to the side and swings his legs out before I stop him with a hand on his shoulder.

"Go? Where the hell do you think you're going? You're human, Jered. And we need you healthy, strong, and sound. How long has it been since you've slept?"

"Two days? Maybe three? I don't know."

I sigh. Maybe we should do this now. Kitra thinks Cephas has Lee. She won't come looking. I've seen to it the brute stays in his room for the rest of the day.

"Call them here," I say. "Both Mir and Lee. You own them both."

"Mira," Jered says uncertainly. "Leela?" Her name is the sound of pain and longing coming from his lips.

They appear before us, Lee still hollow. "She can stay with you now and still be fulfilling the command. You are one of her ma...you have her stone." I wave a hand over the lead handcuffs behind her back before he can see them. "You can retract all the commands, Jered."

"Leela, please be yourself again." He utters the words like a prayer. He waits, his chest rising and falling faster with each breath.

Her face melts. So does her body. She falls onto the bed, across his lap, sobbing. I squeeze my eyes shut as Jered runs his hand lovingly over her back. She continues for a long time, until she finally runs out of tears. I open my eyes to see him stroking her hair, inches from her face.

"I thought you were dead. Or...or worse," she says.

"Nothing could stop me from coming for you, Leela." She lets out a sound somewhere between a laugh and a cry, and he smiles, still staring intently in her eyes.

"You called me," she says. "That means—"

"I have your stone. Cephas and Achan now have fakes."

She throws her arms around him and buries her face in his neck. He holds her tight, rocking her gently. Stroking her back. His face is hard, lined with worry far beyond his years while she cannot see it. Mira and I exchange looks.

"Kitra—" Lee says.

"Will lose her hold on you as well." Jered melts as she pulls back to gaze at him again.

He strokes her cheek and leans in for a kiss, so light it is like a whisper. My stomach flips. What is wrong with me?

"I won't let her hurt you anymore," Jered says, touching his forehead to hers.

"I don't care, I just want you to be—"

"Safe? I will be, Leela. I promise."

"If you two are done completing each other's sentences, Jered needs some serious sleep. I suppose you don't mind keeping an eye on him?" Lee smiles at me, eyes still glistening with tears.

"You have to let him sleep though." Mira wags a finger at her.

"I promise to be good." Jered holds up one hand and places his other over his heart.

Mira and I leave the two lovebirds alone. I frown at her as I lock the door behind me.

"What is it?" she asks.

"I don't know. Something still doesn't feel right."

She shrugs. "Kitra has our stones."

"No. It's more than that," I say. "It's Jered. Something is wrong with him. He won't tell me what happened after he was taken. And he's acting a little...funny."

"Funny?" Her forehead wrinkles as she considers the word.

"Strange. Not his usual strange either. He keeps saying he has to go but won't tell me where or why. He seemed so conflicted when it was time to kill Achan."

"It is his father."

"I don't know. Let's just keep an eye on him, okay?"

Mira nods. "Come. We should track Kitra then."

I stop halfway to the throne room, throwing an arm out to stop her in her tracks. "Oh my gods."

"What is it now?" she asks, irritated.

"There were four stones."

"Yes. Four. You, me, Lee, and Brolach."

"What about the others?" My heart races. I stare down the massive hall, sure something is going to pop out from behind one of the stone people and take everything we've just gained away from us.

"Others?" Mira echoes.

She wasn't aware? Kitra did a fabulous job keeping her secret. "I heard there were three others that Kitra kept separate from us. She acquired them when we brought in the magicians."

"That would make sense, but why haven't we seen them? Why

wouldn't she add them to the Council Service?" Mira hugs herself as though she's cold.

"I think she's holding on to them as one of her insurance policies," I say, understanding dawning. "She doesn't want to share." And if she had my loyalty, she'd have a majority if it ever came down to it. Thus all the cloak-and-dagger "let's kill Achan" shit.

"Well, if she does have them, then we'll find their stones and free them too."

I nod my agreement, but my stomach is very unsettled. Mira moves to go again, and I throw my arm out once more.

"Taj!"

"Sophie." My head starts to spin. "Mir, you don't think she—"

"Oh."

I thought I'd sent her on a fool's errand. Something to keep her occupied while we took care of the real bad guys.

Only maybe I didn't.

33

THE ORDER

"You told her to find any secret hiding places in the castle," Mir says, catching on.

"I know what I told her. I have to find her. If she really does find them first..." I can't finish the sentence.

"I will watch Kitra. You go," Mira says.

Without another thought, I begin searching. Flying through the castle beyond human speed. Reaching out with all my senses, searching for her. I am about to give up when I see something in the dungeons. Something small, with a brilliant golden aura, tucked into the corner.

I materialize beside her, and she turns with a gasp, hands outstretched, inches from the stone wall. It is the same spot she dropped through with Gabe over a year ago, just before taking my stone from Kitra.

"Hello," I say, relaxing at the sight of her alone and unharmed.

"Taj!" She hugs me and begins speaking excitedly, stumbling over her own words. "There are people in there. You were right—there is a secret room. Well, it isn't really a room. It's just the hole Gabe opened but with both sides sealed. And now they're in there. I think they're Djinn!"

"Slow down, darling. You say there are Djinn trapped in here?" I touch the wall.

"I was about to let them out."

"There must be lead in there," I say under my breath.

"I can save them, Taj. Don't worry."

A deep voice comes from behind. "I'm going to have to insist that you don't."

I turn in surprise, raising my hands to strike, but he is faster, and I find myself bound to the wall with lead shackles. How could I be so careless? Though in truth, I had no reason to expect Ray to show up.

"This is a fine way to say thank you. I'm beginning to think this is how you greet all Djinn."

He smiles the same dreamboat smile he gave to Qadira when we rescued her. Not really feelin' the love right now, though. "Taj, please just relax."

"Oh yeah, no problem, just chain me to a wall, and I can settle in for a nap. Got any cushions?" I'm doing it to distract him from Sophie. But it's no good. As she darts out to the side, he reaches out and grabs her arm, pulling her back to him and covering her mouth with his free hand. I struggle against my bonds, but it's like an ant trying to move a car. *He cannot hurt her.*

"Sleep," he tells her and eases her to the floor as she falls. I do relax a little. He didn't kill her. Maybe he'll let her go.

"What are you doing here?" I note his simple modern clothing and obvious lack of a collar.

"Trying to save your ass."

Likely story. "I must say you are doing a bang-up job. Don't suppose you work with a Djinni named Rachim?"

He smiles. "I *am* Rachim. Ray for short."

"*You*?" Shit, I'm chained to the wall by a psychopath who's hell bent on killing Djinn.

"You've heard of me?" he asks, moving forward. "Relax. I need you to listen before you go rushing in. Okay?"

"What are you talking about?" I stop struggling against the lead bonds and still, breathing heavily.

Before he can respond, Leela appears between us, facing me. Her face drops, and she raises her hands to release me. She doesn't see him right behind her. I shout out, but it's no good. She's chained right next to me in a flash, and I beat my head into the wall.

"Who are you?" she asks him.

"Lee, this is Rachim. Rachim, Lee. Rachim was just explaining why chaining me to the wall is a good thing."

Her gaze darts to Sophie's sleeping figure in alarm, but I widen my eyes. *Don't.* She clamps her mouth shut.

"Look, I want to let you go, but you're both still slaves. I can't trust you. Same with them." He nods toward the wall.

"Who?" Leela chooses this of all times to be calm.

"Three Djinn trapped inside. They are Kitra's reserve army," I explain. "Aren't you supposed to be somewhere else?"

"Jered sent me away. Told me to stay with you. Said he thought it was safest."

"That boy needs to keep his mouth closed," I say.

"Shut up!" Rachim shouts.

Uh-oh. Yeah. Let's not get Psycho all riled up. We both comply, turning back to him. And he starts pacing.

"Dira insisted we come looking for you after the shock wore off. It was only fair. But the Order wouldn't agree. So it's just me. I told her I would only come if she stayed where it's safe."

Where? Back in the basement?

"Uh-huh," I say. Keep him talking while I think.

"So it's just me. And there's what? Like a thousand magicians here? And how many Djinn under their control?"

"Four of us not inside there," Lee says, and I really wish I could make her stop speaking again, just for a minute.

"Right. Four. Well, two down."

"You need to leave," I say. "We're handling this. It can only be dangerous for you."

"Yeah, you look like you're handling it just fine." He tilts his head. Great, he's got a sense of humor like mine.

"Look, Rachim, I know what you are." I see no sense in pretending.

He stops and raises his eyebrows in question.

"You're the Djinn killer."

Lee gasps.

"What? Are you insane?" he says. "You were there when we saved Dira."

"Well, I highly doubt Rachim is a common Djinn name. You are the fellow keeping tabs on all Djinn passing back and forth through the curtain, no?"

His face goes white. "Well, yeah. I am. But—"

"Everyone except you."

"Yes, but—"

"You want to permanently close the door between worlds."

"Will you please let me talk?" he shouts, spittle flying from his mouth.

I do.

He presses his eyes closed and draws a deep breath as though steadying himself. "Okay. That's me. But it's not what you think. I came out to see what life in the human world is like. That was about eighty years ago, and that's when I met Qadira. My life would never be the same without her."

"Then why try to shut the door?"

"It's safer for everyone," he says easily. I can see by the way his chest puffs up that he's used to debating this issue. He's probably quite good at bringing others over to his side. Of course, we bring new meaning to the term "captive audience."

"But it's okay for *you* to go back and forth." *Go ahead and kill me, but I am not going to cower.*

"No. I'd stay on this side. See, Taj, if you close the door, we lose our immortality. Probably much of our power too. But then we can truly live as humans."

"What?" Lee asks. Her voice is eager, and I want to throttle her.

Psycho's encouraged. He starts speaking more animatedly, making eye contact with Lee. "That's right. We can give a time limit. Have everyone choose where they belong. Let them test it out if they want. Then we close the door and live out our choice."

"I can be human?" Lee breathes the words like a prayer.

"Lee—"

"Of course you can. It's what we all want, isn't it? All of us who've crossed over. And if we lose some of our power, our immortality, then they will stop hunting us down."

"The Order?" I ask.

"Magicians! Why would the Order do that? I thought you knew. The Order is a group of free Djinn that are working toward peaceful assimilation here on Earth. We keep a database of all members, so we can watch and help if anyone is taken by a magician against their will."

"So you...free Djinn?" Lee asks, hope springing to her eyes. "You've done this before. You're here to save us."

"Um, Lee. I hate to burst your bubble, but he's the guy who chained us to the wall." I rattle one of the chains against the stone to make my point.

"You have to be neutralized. It's the first rule of acquisitions. You wouldn't mean to harm or impede my rescue attempt, but you may not be able to help yourself."

How very sweet.

"Okay, let's say all of this is true." He looks relieved. "Then tell me why you've been going around killing Djinn."

34

OCTOBER 18, 1866

I'VE BEEN CALLED TO MY MASTER'S SIDE, AND I BETRAY NO REACTION WHEN I find a swollen and bruised Pierce nearby. Charlotte cries softly on the bed, and somehow, I don't think the tears are for me.

"The other Djinni," Lucas begins. "Madame Wilde is his master?"

"Yes." My pulse speeds up, but I remain impassive. Why is he asking about Cal?

"Pierce and I have come to an agreement," he says. "You can relax by the way. I do not blame you for striking him. It was idiotic for him to approach you without my protection."

"Thank you, Master Lucas." I do not let on that my reaction had nothing to do with fear of retribution.

"We both know we want power. We both cannot have it. Not when we are so close in proximity and not when we have only one Djinni."

"Very sensible of you, Master."

He waves me off. "It is dangerous for Lottie's mother to be in possession of such a creature."

Dangerous for him.

"You will kill the Widow Wilde and make it look like natural causes. An illness perhaps. Then give the stone to Pierce."

Charlotte's sobs intensify. My heart skips a beat.

"Master." *I use my most sincere and subservient voice.*

Pierce looks about to strike, but Lucas holds up a hand to hold him off. He cocks his head, ready to hear me.

"I do not recommend this. You should know that in order to protect his master, Caldor will do whatever is necessary. He will kill me if he needs to, and then neither of you will have a Djinni."

"I thought you couldn't die." *Pierce raises his eyebrows.*

"It would be difficult to manage it, but you three almost succeeded a few months ago."

"Then we must distract him. How can we do this?" *Lucas asks.*

This is not what I hoped for, but I must answer. "Charlotte can give him commands."

All eyes turn to the girl with bright-red eyes, and she looks at me mutinously. I've just taken her only possible recourse. Her only way out of the hell she's found herself in. Worse than that, I've betrayed the only man I've ever truly loved.

But a command is a command.

"Call him here and make him go to the gazebo," *Lucas says.* "Tell him to do it right away. Be careful how you word it, or I will chain you to that bed and never let you leave or utter another sound."

"Taj," *he continues, turning to me.* "Be ready in case she finds some mischief."

I nod, but my mind is very far away, once again reliving the torture I was forced to inflict on Lee all those years ago. I cannot hurt Caldor.

"Cal," *Charlotte calls.*

Instantly, he is by her side. Cal gazes around nervously, searching my eyes when he spots me, neutral on the outside, screaming internally. I cannot move. Cannot breathe. For if I do, I will surely fall to pieces.

"Cal, you will go immediately to the gazebo in the woods and wait inside it for me." *Charlotte's words find a way through her tears, and Caldor takes one more distraught look at me before disappearing.*

"Now?" *Lucas asks me. And with that one word, he's managed to avoid the one possible caveat, the one last hope that this won't go the way he wants it to.*

My lips move. I cannot delay the response. "Wait for the lead to seep into his system. A half hour ought to do it. Then he will be unable to respond if his master calls for him."

35

TRUST

Rachim shakes his head sadly and turns to walk away. "I'm wasting time. I need to go. If all goes well, you'll be free by the end of the day, and we can talk then."

The door at the top of the stairs clangs shut with such finality I wince.

"Sophie," I say.

Lee's starting to fade from exposure to the lead. She's had a lot more than I have of late. Her head droops, her hair, uncut for so long, shadowing her face from view, and I swallow. This is not good. Not good at all.

"Sophie!" I scream. When I'm done, I bang my head into the wall again and squeeze my eyes shut. My chest feels heavy, and my skin crawls with the burn of the lead. That exertion cost me. He's got her under a spell. There's no way I'm going to be able to wake her by yelling.

I open my eyes, forcing myself to focus, to stay sharp. I have to do something. I look around. There's nothing here but hay, dirt, torches, stone, and metal. I lick my lips, trying to fend off the cloud that's starting to settle on my vision. The prickling sensation of a million pins in my flesh doesn't help.

"Lee," I whisper, reaching as far as my restraint will allow. The metal sizzles against my wrist, and smoke crawls up into the air away from it. I ignore the agony and stretch my fingers out as far as they will go. Until I think my hand will break. Finally, I manage to brush against her hand, and I focus all my energy into zapping her awake.

She screeches a little, and her head snaps upward.

"Touch my finger. We have to link."

She reaches over just an inch, but enough to allow me to crook my index finger around hers.

"I can't, Taj," she moans. "So much lead already."

"We need to wake Sophie."

"I can't."

"If we don't, someone else will find her here with us. Do you want that someone to be Cephas? Achan?"

I hate being the cause of more pain, but it does the trick. She focuses her energy with mine, and I will the child to wake.

Sophie's eyes flutter open just as Lee's hand slips away, limp. I force my eyes open and work the muscles around my mouth, trying to speak. But nothing's coming out. And my body feels like it's been dropped in a vat of acid.

As the edges of my vision turn black, the restraints recede, and I slide toward the ground, vaguely aware that it's going to hurt. But instead I slow, as though a bungee cord has hold of me, and land softly next to Lee, who moans a little.

Sophie runs to me and throws herself on top of me, knocking us both to the ground after all.

"Ouch."

She giggles. Figures. I right myself as the last of the pain subsides and find Lee struggling to a sitting position. I go to her, let my magic speed her healing. She must have really been exposed to a lot of lead to be this bad off so long after being released.

"We have to find Jered," I say, helping her to her feet.

"What? Why?"

"If Rachim is telling the truth, which I doubt, he doesn't know about the fakes. Or—"

"That Jered's our master!" Lee exclaims. "He'll think he has to kill him." She grasps the front of my vest with both fists and shakes me lightly.

And if he's lying, Jered will be able to identify him. Either way, Jered dies. I look at Lee's frightened face and regret even the part I did speak out loud. She doesn't know he was ever taken.

"You cannot go to him," I say instead.

"Oh no. Why did he order me away?" She's begun to cry now, pent-up leftovers from the month she's spent as an emotional vegetable, I suppose.

"Trying to be gallant and protect you again, I suspect. Idiot doesn't realize it never ends well when he does that."

Lee stops crying to glare at me. *Better*.

"Stay with Sophie. Protect her."

"I'll let the others out now," Sophie says, stepping toward the wall.

"No!" Lee and I both reach out our hands to stop her.

"I'm not sure that's the best idea," I say. "They're under Kitra's control, and we don't know anything about them. We should ride this out first."

"You sound like *him*," Sophie says, hands on her hips. "I heard everything, you know. Even through my sleep."

"You never cease to amaze me," I say. "But in this case, the psycho had a point."

Sophie continues to pout at me as I turn to Lee. "Keep an eye on her, please." And I disappear. I'll have to trust them to do the right thing.

JERED AND BROLACH

I REACH OUT AGAIN, THIS TIME SIFTING THROUGH THE HUDDLED MASSES FOR a sign of Jered. Mira, I see, is still babysitting Kitra. No sign anywhere of Rachim. I have only an hour before we are all due in the throne room for Council Service. Then the jig is up. So to speak.

The Djinn signature is easier to find than a single distinct aura among hundreds. Maybe Brolach can help me search. But I see, as I appear in the center of the bedroom, that he's already found Jered. Or perhaps that Jered's already found him. Either way, something is very, very wrong. Time slows.

Jered's hands are raised, holding what appears to be a ball of blue lightning, his face strained with concentration. Brolach throws out his own hand with a blast that would kill Jered if he weren't his master. I don't plan on taking any chances with Lee's heart though, so I erect a wall of energy between the two of them, and Brolach's attack bounces back at him, knocking him off his feet.

"Stop!" I yell, and both of them look at me.

Jered's still poised to throw his silly little ball, and Brolach is spread-eagle on the floor, looking rather enticing. I leave my force field up and step between them.

"What is going on up here?"

Neither one says a word. So I draw a deep breath and continue.

"Fine. Don't tell me. But while you two are trying to kill each other, there are—what? Millions of lives at stake. So suck it up and get with the program. We have two hours to take down Her Royal Pain in the Ass. Meanwhile, she has three other Djinn under her control, locked away in a lead-lined compartment downstairs. Oh, and there's a Djinn murdering psychopath on the loose." *Breathe.*

"But—" Jered starts.

"Did something happen?" Brolach asks, raising his palm in the air to stay Jered.

"Why, yes, thank you for asking. Rachim showed up. He stuck Lee and me to the wall with lead restraints and is attempting to free everyone, or so he says. Trouble is, he's bound to kill Jered doing it."

"Rachim?" Jered asks, placing a hand against the wall before him.

"That's the killer's name," I say.

Brolach looks downright frightened. Poor dear. He's so sensitive, after all. Well, except when he's trying to kill Jered. Not that he could have succeeded, of course.

"It's okay," I say, placing a hand on his elbow and pulling him toward me. "I'm taking him out the moment I lay eyes on him."

I'm rewarded with another heart-stopping grin.

"Um, Taj..." Jered clears his throat.

I snap, and the wall dissolves, letting him stumble forward.

"Leela." Jered grasps my arm in desperation.

"Is down in the dungeon with Sophie. She's fine. Though your little stunt to keep her safe didn't help."

Jered narrows his eyes and darts his gaze over to Brolach, and when I look, the latter appears ready to cry.

"Taj, I should have you go and protect Leela."

"Don't be ridiculous." I wave him off. "The only way to protect her is to free her from Kitra's control."

"He's right, Master," Brolach says. And I smile. "Kitra is the priority here. The rest will have to be sorted out later."

I draw him to me, unable to stand it, and press my lips to his. He reaches his arms around me, running them up my back, and I sigh against his mouth.

"I'm going to end this," Jered says.

I pull away and turn to find him, eyes locked on us.

"We need to stick together."

"No. I'm going now. You stay here with him." Damn him. He gave me a command.

"Jered! Don't be an idiot. If you blow this—"

I'm cut off by the door slamming in my face. Great.

"Taj." Brolach takes my hand and tugs me over to him. "I'm afraid something is wrong with our young master."

"No shit."

"I think whatever Rachim did to him has left him unbalanced. He said...he said..." Brolach's eyes glaze with tears, and he places the back of his hand to his mouth.

I gather him into my arms, kiss his neck tenderly. "What did he say, dearest?"

"He was so angry. He accused me of doing all those horrible things, Taj. He was going to kill me. I had to try—you don't believe him, do you?" He pulls away, looking frightened again.

"Of course not. If I thought you had, I would have killed you, not kissed you."

He seems to deflate before me. "I was so scared. If you hadn't come, he would have done it. My magic would have never hit the mark, but I had to try to defend myself."

"Shh..." I pull him back into my arms and press my lips to his ear. "Jered would not have killed you, Brolach."

"You didn't see him, Taj."

"I know him," I say. But in my mind, I watch Jered's face filled with rage as he pushes the tip of his rapier through Cephas's chest. Whatever Rachim did to him, I'm going to have to undo. But I can't until Kitra is finished.

"What do we do now?" he asks.

"Well, I cannot go anywhere. I've been commanded to stay here with you. So either Jered will succeed and come for us, or Kitra will kill him and we will show up for Council Service. I'd say we have a bit of a wait though either way. Any suggestions?"

I breathe the last word over his ear and feel him tremble against me. Mmm. I know I could use a little de-stressing. The next thing I know, he's kissing me, and I'm lost in his scent and the feel of his body against mine.

My mind wanders back to Leela in the dungeon with Sophie. Jered facing Kitra. Mira. And I can't concentrate. I pull back with a sigh.

"Is something wrong?" he asks.

"It isn't you, gorgeous. I just can't do this while I'm worried about them."

"Oh. I understand." I hear his disappointment.

"I feel so helpless," I admit.

"Nonsense," he says, squeezing my shoulder. "You could never be helpless, Taj."

"Then what do you call this?" I ask, miserable. I can't remember the last time I actually admitted my feelings to anyone. Well, that's not exactly true either. It was on the rooftop of a Chicago hotel. With Lee.

"I call it 'lucky me,'" he says with a grin. "Because as selfish as it is, I feel much safer with you here."

37

OCTOBER 18, 1866

I FULLY BELIEVE THE WIDOW WILDE UNDERSTANDS WHY I HAVE COME. I'VE killed many humans over the years on command. Most of them deserve it. She is no exception. It is the maiming, torture, and enslavement that I have a problem with. Is that wrong?

I sit on the edge of the bed and smile at her. She doesn't return the gesture. But neither does she scream or call for help.

"I take it I will find Caldor incapacitated?"

"Yes."

"I see. So she's done it then? Decided her mother is in the way?"

Ah. She does not see. "I do not belong to your daughter any longer," I say, and for the first time, I see some emotion in her cold gray eyes. "She survives. It is her betrothed that claims me now."

"Lucas is a magician?" she asks under her breath.

"Only recently."

She opens her mouth, thinks better of it, and closes it again.

"It will not hurt."

"Thank you." Then. "Taj? Will you do me a favor? I know I can hardly hope to ask for such a thing, but I must try."

"What do you desire?" I've never heard such words uttered from the mouth of a magician.

"*Try to help her when you can. Keep an eye on her. Protect her,*" she pleads with me, her frozen exterior cracking. She grasps my hand and holds it to her heart. "*Everything I've ever done, I've done for her.*"

"*I will watch her,*" I say.

She is smiling when she dies. Her heart stops beating, and I lay her gently down on the bed. I said it to ease her mind. But it was a lie.

Clutching the stone in my hand, wishing I could somehow accidentally crush it and free Cal, I reappear before the three young magicians.

Without a word, I hand the stone to Lucas, who studies it for a moment before handing it to Pierce.

"*Caldor!*" he shouts at the top of his lungs.

He appears in the center of the room and, to his credit, does nothing to reveal the confusion I am certain is gripping him right now. I remember it well. The call from a new master. The only thing with the power to draw you even from a prison of lead. I watch as he takes in the sight of Pierce clutching his stone. He shakes a stray curl from his eyes, searching for understanding among the faces in the room. His gaze lands on me.

"*Master. What is your bidding?*"

"*I trust you will uphold your end of the bargain?*" Lucas says, stepping between them.

"*I will leave. I want to get out of this depressing state now anyway,*" Pierce agrees. "*Come here, Caldor.*"

Caldor steps forward, and Pierce pulls him to his side with a tug.

"*We're going to have a lot of fun together, you and I,*" he says, pressing his fingers into Caldor's arm so hard I see him wince. "*Let's start with Europe. I've always wondered what it's like out there. How about you make me a little castle in England?*"

"*Yes, Master.*" Caldor's eyes penetrate my very soul with such sudden venom, I find myself gasping out loud. And as he raises his arms to fulfill his command, he leaves one last statement ringing in the air.

"*I will find you again one day, Taj.*"

I am not sure whether to take it as a promise or a threat. I'm not sure which is more painful.

38

TORN

BROLACH HAS SUCCEEDED IN DRAWING MY MIND AWAY FROM MY SITUATION BY working on the tension in my shoulders and back. Somehow I find myself kissing him again. I suppose it might have something to do with me taking hold of his wrists and pulling him down on the bed beside me.

"Taj. Leela. Brolach." Kitra's voice rings in my head, and I have only a split second to disentangle myself from him before we appear before her throne.

I kneel hastily along with the others, breathing heavily and trying desperately to calm my arousal. *Think of Kitra naked*, I tell myself. That helps.

"It seems somehow our young friend here"—Kitra pulls Lee up by her hair—"has managed to break her command and slip away from all three of us."

I glance to the side to see Achan and Cephas seated on their own golden thrones. Looks like we're out of time. Where's Jered? I cringe with the realization that our fates lie in the hands of a twenty-two-year-old kid who's been brainwashed by a maniac.

"I thought I'd made it quite impossible," Kitra is saying. Lee's doing a decent job staying impassive, but I know it cannot last. "But you've fooled

me before. So out with it. How did you manage it? And what did you do?"
She shakes Lee roughly and waits.

"Master Kitra, I was fulfilling a command." She nods to Kitra's right,
and I glance sidelong at Cephas to find his face blank. She's manipulating
his memories. Of course she can. Nice. She was commanded, just not
by him.

"I sent her," Cephas agrees, drawing Kitra's attention. "To find a slave
to bring to my quarters." Now he's the one lying, not Lee.

"Then why did you not tell me when I summoned you?" Kitra roars at
him, throwing Lee to the ground at our feet.

Uh-oh.

"I do not have to answer to you," Cephas says, standing. I see Lee's
mouth moving slightly as she places the words in his mouth.

"You are trying to cause an argument between us, aren't you?" Kitra
hisses at Lee.

"No, Master. I would never."

"Come up here."

Lee rises and floats up onto the dais with Kitra. She appears unfeel-
ing, except for the slight tremor in her hands, now clasped behind her
back.

"I believe it is time for some punishment," Kitra says. "Public humilia-
tion should help." She runs a finger down Lee's cheek, eliciting a shiver.

"Taj, bind our little Leela in lead chains in the center of the room. I
want you to televise this. Project it to every room in the castle."

I wave a hand, and it is done. I sincerely wish Jered would hurry. I
can't imagine what is keeping him. He should have been here long before
us. Unless. Unless Rachim...

Kitra pulls a lead pipe from the air and begins circling Lee, who now
dangles by her wrists from the ceiling. She raises it in the air like a base-
ball bat, and Lee's eyes snap shut, waiting for the whoosh of air before the
strike. But Kitra holds, an evil smile rolling across her mouth.

"No. No, I think it will be more meaningful coming from someone
else. Tell me, Leela, which of these Djinn are you closest to?"

Her eyes open and meet mine. "Taj."

"Taj," Kitra calls. "Deal Leela her punishment, and don't be too gentle." She hands me the pipe, changing the bottom to a plastic grip, so I will not burn my hands. "I will shield you with my magic so you will not be harmed," she whispers in my ear. "You failed me, Taj. Achan lives. This is just as much for you as for her."

I swallow back the lump in my throat and adjust my sweaty grip. *Any moment now would be good, Jered.* Any moment. But he isn't coming. And my hands jerk to fulfill their command.

I swing the pipe against her legs, deciding at the last moment that this will cause the least damage. It hits with a sickening *thud*, and a whimper escapes her lips. Tears burn at my eyes as I pull it back for another swing.

"The stomach is a tender spot," Kitra says, staying my hand. "Let's try that next, shall we? And let it stand in contact with her skin for a while before preparing for the next strike."

Wonderful. Kitra can teach an Internet class on proper torture techniques. She removes her hand, and I move to fulfill my command. My body shakes with sobs, and I can barely see through my tears. Though Lee's doing a great job keeping it together.

"Hold, Taj."

My eyes press closed, squeezing a last tear from my lids. *About time, kid.* My hands tremble with the pressure to fulfill both masters' commands. I manage to stay my position through sheer force of will.

"What is the meaning of this?" Kitra asks.

"Mira, incapacitate Cephas and Achan." Jered strides forward to meet us in the center of the room.

Kitra's laugh dies on her lips when Mira rises, throwing out her hands. Thick iron chains shoot out of each of their chairs, binding them so tight, it would be impossible for anyone to move. Mira clasps her hands together, and both men are gagged as well.

"How is this possible?" Kitra asks. "Mira should not be able to attack her masters."

"They aren't her masters." Jered grins. "I am." He pulls Cephas's corded necklace from beneath his shirt, and Kitra gasps.

"But I am still in possession of their stones," Kitra says, like she isn't terribly sure.

"Not for long," Jered answers.

He pulls a gun from the air, and I raise an eyebrow. I hope he knows how to use that thing. He looks pretty confident at least. And Kitra backs away a few steps.

"Taj, let Leela down. Lose the weapon."

I feel Kitra's protection snap away, but I am fast. The pipe disappears, and Leela falls to the ground, where I steady her with my hands about her waist.

"Hand over the stones, Kitra. It's over," Jered says.

Shoot her, you moron.

Kitra tucks her hands in her sleeves and smiles. "Fine then." But when her hands come out, it is only her aura that she throws toward Jered.

He squeezes the trigger, and my hand flicks automatically, crushing the gun into a twisted lump of metal. My command to always protect her. Thankfully, Lee has done the same for Jered and blocked Kitra's spell with her magic.

"It seems," says Kitra, shaking with barely controlled rage, "we are at an impasse, Jered."

"Let's fight it out hand to hand then," he says, returning her grin.

"Taj, kill him," she commands.

My hand springs to life.

"Taj, no!" Jered shouts.

And I am stilled.

"Do not harm me, any of you," Jered says quickly. "Protect me," he adds, seeing the power gathering at Kitra's fingertips.

The two magicians circle each other at a distance of about ten yards. Fingers crackling with energy. A thin layer of moisture glistens on Jered's forehead. And I notice, for the first time, what looks like dried blood coating his left hand.

"Incapacitate him," Kitra yells, copying Jered's command regarding Cephas and Achan.

"Incapacitate her!" Jered shouts half over her command.

They are both playing with fire. All four of us throw out our hands, ropes and chains springing from the air, wrapping themselves around their bodies. Both magicians tumble to the floor.

"Don't gag me!" Kitra screams.

"Don't—" Jered gets out before a silvery band of material covers his mouth. I don't know who did it. I'm not sure it matters.

Leela runs to him. I try to grab her arm, but she slides from my grip and sinks to her knees over him, reaching for the gag with her hands.

"Freeze," says Kitra. We all comply. Jered's eyes grow large, focused on her face, so close yet so unreachable. "You will no longer protect him," she says.

My heart sinks in my chest. It's over. We must obey both masters so long as they each have our stones.

"Leela, do you love him?" Kitra asks. I'd almost think her voice was kind, if I didn't know her so well.

"Yes," Lee whispers.

"Good. I want you to put your hands around his neck and squeeze until he dies. Now."

Leela begins to sob as she reaches for his neck. Jered remains completely still. I can almost hear his last thoughts, assuring her it isn't her fault.

REAL POWER

"Oh God," Leela sobs as she tightens her fingers against his throat. Choking sounds force their way through his gag, and his eyes roll back in his head. The tips of her fingers turn white with the pressure of her effort. His body twitches against the floor. "No. Please, no," she begs.

My mind slips back to the first time we four held service for the Council. I remember Leela's hand sliding from my own. Her whispering his name in her mind. I recall her appearing in my apartment and meeting his eyes. How her mask of indifference shattered.

My gaze falls on her tortured face. "You can stop, Lee," I say.

For a moment, I'm not sure she understood me. Then she pulls in a gasp, and her fingers tremble, some of their color flooding back as she loosens her hold.

"That's right," I say. "You feel it, don't you?"

Leela draws a deep, shuddering breath and slowly, carefully releases her grip. Angry red bruises color Jered's flesh, and he sucks in what life he can through his nose. Kitra's face falls as Lee yanks the gag from his mouth, hysterical with happiness. Jered gulps at the air with a horrible wheezing sound. But Lee lays her hands on him, and his wounds disappear before my eyes. His bonds loosen and fall away.

"I said kill him, Leela!" Kitra shrieks. "I'll have you both turned into marble statues."

"Brilliant," Jered whispers. He leans into Lee's ear, and she grins.

"Fine. Taj, you kill him," Kitra says.

Jered's head snaps toward me as my hands raise in preparation. But Lee has already pointed both to me and to Kitra. I go down beneath the weight of what feels like a thousand lead chains. I have just enough time, before hitting the floor, to see Kitra's terror-stricken face turn to marble.

No one touches me until all seven stones are retrieved from her petrified body. Which takes some time. Finally, when it is done, and Lee has crushed them into dust, she removes my bonds.

"Next time, do you think you can use a little moderation?" I ask her, conjuring some fresh clothing. My signature tight jeans and a dark T-shirt.

"Sorry, Taj," Lee says, her arm around Jered's waist.

I allow myself a smile and move to embrace them both when Jered falls with a grunt, nearly knocking Leela over. I rush forward to help lower him gently down.

"What's happening?" Leela screams.

"He isn't dead," Rachim says, striding into the room. His hands are linked with three other Djinn. Two men and one woman, all with glowing emerald eyes. But my gaze rests on the Djinni at the end, who holds the limp form of Sophie in the crook of his arm. His is a face I recognize, though I haven't seen it in a hundred and fifty years. And the last time I did, he threatened revenge.

Caldor.

"You don't understand," Lee says to Rachim, covering Jered's body with her own. "He saved us."

"You are saying that because he's commanded you to," Rachim says, though I hear the hesitation in his voice.

"Or maybe you're just a psychopathic murderer here to kill us all." I step in front of Lee and Jered.

Mira and Brolach join me on either side. And I see the others exchange looks.

"If he is truly innocent, you have nothing to worry about," Rachim says smoothly. "All he has to do is give you your freedom."

Mira and Brolach slip their hands in mine, and Lee joins the chain on Mira's side. We stand linked between Rachim and Jered. Four against four.

"Then it seems we won't have a problem," Lee says.

"Give us Sophie," I say, unable to stand it another moment.

Rachim looks around, confused, and then laughs when he sees who I am looking at.

"The little magician?" he asks. "I don't think so."

My eyes burn as green sparks fly out of them and wind whips around my body, blowing my T-shirt back against my chest. When I speak again, it is with a great thundering voice that echoes around the enormous room.

"I said hand her over, Rachim."

"And I said no."

Jered stumbles to his feet behind me.

"Sophie," he says in my ear.

"You don't know who you're dealing with." I address the other three. "This is the Djinni responsible for the murders you felt earlier this month."

The others take a collective gasp, but do not drop hands.

"You are mistaken, Taj," Cal says, shifting Sophie's weight in his arm. "He has freed us."

"No. The magician behind me has freed you. He retrieved your stones at great personal risk."

"Then why are you still bound?" Rachim counters.

"He hasn't had a chance to free us yet," Lee shouts. More wind whips around the room, gathering her hair and spraying it behind her like the tail on Rachim's shooting star tattoo.

"Ray has done nothing to harm us," says the other male.

"Not yet. But he will."

"Taj," Rachim says. His temper flares, as does the electricity surrounding him. "Think. If I was the one responsible, why hasn't anyone else died?"

I swallow hard. Lee glances at me from the corner of her eye.

"It isn't him," Jered says. His voice is soft, but we all hear him.

He steps around our protective wall and out in front of Rachim and his line.

"I don't want to hurt anyone. I never asked to be a Djinn master. Leela and I have fallen in love, and I will do whatever it takes to make sure she's free. Whatever it takes to make sure all of you are."

I believe, this time, Leela's tears are born of pride.

"If that is the case," Rachim says, letting go of the chain and stepping forward to meet him, "then all you have to do is free them right now, and this will all be over."

Jered's face contorts, a deep shade of plum working its way up his neck. His hand shoots to his forehead. The "something" wrong with him is surfacing at a very inopportune moment.

"Just a minute," I say, stepping forward to place a hand on his shoulder. It is a gesture that I hope sends a message to Rachim. I have to give Jered time to get control. "If you're such a great guy, Rachim, why have you kidnapped a child?"

Rachim's head snaps back like I've struck him.

"No one's taken a child," one of the other Djinn says.

"So that's just what? A doll?" I ask, gesturing toward Sophie.

"We haven't taken her—we're protecting her!" says the female. She's tiny, but I can tell from the piercings and spiky hair, she's probably got some spunk.

"From whom?" I demand.

"From *you*," says Caldor, and it's my turn to feel like I've been slapped.

"She saved us from the lead prison," says the other man.

My gaze flies to Sophie when Cal moves, but he simply drops the woman's hand and transfers her tenderly to his other arm.

So Sophie went ahead with her little plan anyway, did she? And now she has more loyal Djinn indebted to her. I relax a bit, letting my shoulders fall.

"Enough!" shouts Rachim. "Free them now or die, human."

Jered's entire body shakes, and I tighten my grip on his shoulder. His face is scrunched up so tight, I think he might explode. "I...I...c-can't."

Lee runs in front of him, taking his arms in her hands, searching his face for answers. She's blocked Rachim for the moment. But he will not have patience forever.

I hold up a hand, asking Rachim to allow us to speak. He purses his lips but waits, folding his arms in front of his chest.

"Jered," I say. "What do you mean you can't?"

He falls to his knees, trembling so hard, I am reminded of a volcano preparing to erupt. Breath comes rapid and shallow through his nose. Lee drops with him, still hanging on for dear life.

"I w-want to, but he won't, he won't—"

My gaze falls on the dried blood still staining his hand, and my head reels. I dive for his arm and yank back his sleeve. Cutting into his skin is a black band of velvet, a single pearl in the center. My gaze darts to Lee, who seems stricken beyond belief. Jered is crying now, unable to look her in the face.

40

OCTOBER 31, 1866

I AM LEAVING MY MASTER'S CHAMBERS WHEN CHARLOTTE PRESSES A PIECE OF parchment into my hand. I am so taken aback by this, I grip her shoulder, turning her to face me. She shakes her head, touching her throat, and I understand. She still may not speak without either Lucas's presence or permission.

I unfold the piece of paper, staring at the smudged ink. Obviously this was written in haste. Most likely she is taking quite a chance. I could easily go right to my master, her new husband, and reveal this newfound mode of communication.

If I bear his child, he will be forced to give me more freedom. He will learn to trust me. But I've tried, with both body and magic, to conceive and have failed. Will you help me?

With one toss into the air, the parchment disappears, and Charlotte watches me with some relief. She opens her hands in a question and waits.

"No," I say. "I am sorry, but I do not believe this will help you as you hope."

Her face contorts in an expression of pain, and she falls at my feet, grasping my coattails. I pry off her hands as gently as possible and scoop her into my arms. She presses her face to my chest and lets her tears soak through.

I lay her on the bed and turn to go, but she grabs my arm and pulls me back toward her. With a heavy sigh, I sit on the side of the bed, and she curls into my side, clinging for dear life.

"*What is it you want from me?*" *I ask. All I want to do is be free to mourn Cal.*

I guess I shouldn't have because she reaches up, and before I know what's happening, she's kissing me. It would appear she's learned a thing or two since our first such encounter. But I take her wrists in my hands, plucking them from around my neck, and push her away with enough force to make it clear I'm not interested.

"*That won't do it,*" *I say, amused.* "*I've never known a Djinni and human to mate successfully. I don't even know if it's possible.*"

She glares at me murderously as I let go of her arms. I fully expect her to slap me again, but instead she begins to cry. Oh, for the love all things female. I scoot her into my side again and let her empty herself of all tears.

When she stifles her tears, I tip her chin up and smile. "*You don't want me, Charlotte,*" *I say.* "*You want freedom. I'm just sorry I cannot help you.*"

She begins shaking her head emphatically. All right, no. No what? I try to convey my confusion with my expression, and she purses her lips. Then she climbs onto her knees, throws her arms around me, and presses her face to mine again.

I'm knocked backward onto the bed as she moves against me. I watch her aura cover us, and before I can react, we're both completely nude. She straddles me and kisses her way down my neck.

As calmly as I can, I shove her off me and stand, covering us both with a single snap. What is wrong with her?

"*Charlotte,*" *I say.* "*Perhaps I wasn't clear. I am not interested. I never really was. I mean you no offense, but you just aren't my type.*"

That's when she begins throwing things at me. Whatever's in reach. Pillows, vases, picture frames, jewelry. After the first item, I place a wall of energy between us so that everything bounces harmlessly off.

Laughter rings from behind, and I spin to find Lucas leaning casually against the doorframe, his red-blond hair flopping enticingly in his eye. Charlotte stops throwing things and crosses her arms defiantly.

"*You see, my darling? You failed miserably. I told you he was loyal.*"

Ah. I see now.

"*I would have earned my freedom,*" *she whispers.*

"And I would have earned a lifetime of misery," I say. "Not to say you aren't worth it. Well, yes, I suppose that's exactly what I'm saying."

"I've never met a man who didn't want me," she says now, standing and coming as close as possible without hitting my makeshift wall.

"Well, with all due respect, I'm not exactly a man."

Lucas slaps me on the back, squeezing my shoulder. "You've earned one request, Taj. Within reason, of course."

"You'll spoil him," Charlotte warns.

"You would know," I say.

Lucas laughs again. "I believe in treating Taj the same way my daddy treated our slaves. See, Lottie, you catch more flies with honey than with vinegar. So what'll it be?" he asks me.

I surprise myself when the words come out.

"Let Charlotte go."

41

WILL MEETS MAGIC

Lee strokes Jered's face with her hands, shushing him softly. "It's okay," she says. "It's okay."

"I tried to cut off my hand." Jered's voice quakes as much as the rest of him. "I couldn't get past the skin."

"This isn't his fault." I look up at Rachim, whose face is unreadable. "You set us up! You commanded him not to turn the stones over so that you could kill him."

"That's ridiculous," he says. "If I wanted to, I could kill him anytime."

"It isn't him," Jered says, grabbing my shirt with his fist and pulling me down to his quivering face.

I sense he's trying to tell me something.

But how do I know that it isn't just another command? He swallows hard, pleading with his eyes for me to understand. Then I remember, and I feel the blood drain from my face. He sees this and lets go of his grip, allowing me to stumble backward.

I turn toward Mira and Brolach. Mira's face is impassive as she continues to hold his hand, ready for whatever action is necessary. Brolach's eyes meet mine, and I know. I know I have indeed been played.

"He accused me of doing all those horrible things, Taj. He was going to kill me. I had to try—you don't believe him, do you?" Well, I do now.

Fool me once, shame on you. Fool me twice, you need to die.

"But you have his stone," I say to Jered, without taking my eyes off Brolach. "I know. I thought that was it. But it doesn't work that way. His magic is so strong. I was able to stop from killing Achan. I was testing whether I could resist since I had the stone. I did it, but it cost me, and then he found out I had it, and I couldn't. I couldn't." He can't finish.

A cold sweat sweeps over my flesh, and the hair on my arms and neck stands on end. It never occurred to me that the roles could be reversed. Djinn enslaving humans? I suppose it makes sense—our magic is stronger. But why would anyone do that? And to one of the few humans that doesn't deserve it. I feel a wave of nausea as a myriad of emotions pass through me: anger, heartbreak, despair.

"Hey," I say, placing a hand on his shoulder. "It's okay, kid. You've been great. Don't try to fight it. Not now. Then it won't hurt so much."

"He's right," Leela says. "It's okay. We know. We know."

"Why?" I ask Brolach.

Mira catches on and drops his hand like a hot poker.

He moves closer, and I hold up a hand, ready to strike if necessary. He's surrounded, so why does he look so damn smug? He certainly doesn't look nervous or unsure anymore.

"Why what? Why did I lie? Because if you'd figured it out too early, I wouldn't have been able to use you to get to the others before I kill you."

Okay, that hurt. But I'm sure as hell not going to let him know it.

"It's over now," I say. "Let him go."

"I don't think so. See, all I really needed was for Kitra to lose her hold over you all. I control you because I control Jered."

"Have you forgotten about the rest of us?" Rachim says, and the other three step forward menacingly. I really wish Caldor would put Sophie down.

"Not in the least," Brolach says.

My gaze falls on the clothes of the three musketeers. Long sleeves. All of them. Shit. My heart pounds against my rib cage because I know what's going to happen. "So you control them too," I say, trying to head it off.

Leela looks over, shocked. Brolach nods, and the others pull up their sleeves to reveal matching bracelets as I'd feared. It would have been all too easy with them incapacitated if he knew the location. Just make Jered follow along to shield him with his aura from the lead. And I gave Brolach the freedom to do it because of my deal with Kitra. I shake myself a little and try to focus.

But *Sophie*. Rachim looks positively stunned. Mira edges toward me, and I ignore her, trying not to bring attention to the movement. Lee still hangs on to Jered for dear life.

Brolach snaps his fingers, and Rachim is bound in chains of lead. He falls to his knees, and I reach out, but there's nothing I can do. Mira slips her hand in mine. I take a deep breath, trying to keep my head clear. I've never seen so many Djinn gathered in this world. It's unnerving, and the very air sizzles with the power of it, which does nothing to ease my mind.

"Give me the stones, Jered," Brolach says, holding out a hand.

Lee tightens her grip, and Jered begins shaking once again. I lick my lips. *Think, Taj*. Jered has Brolach's stone, but he said that Brolach's magic was stronger. He's definitely fighting it, though it appears to be a losing battle. He managed not to kill Achan, but that was before Brolach was paying attention. What's stronger than a Djinni? I glance at Lee, clutching his face in her hands, forcing him to look her in the eyes, feeding him her strength.

"You don't have to listen, Jered," I say. Everyone stares at me like I'm suffering dementia, but I continue. "Leela broke the spell. She stopped the command three times now. And each one," I say, being sure to glance between them, "was because of her love for you."

Jered's eyes grow large, taking in Lee's face. She smiles through her steady stream of tears and nods.

"Love is more powerful," I say. But I'm not sure. Lee is Djinn, fighting a magician's hold. Jered's situation is reversed. But maybe, with the stone...

Jered draws a deep, shuddering breath and focuses everything on Lee.

Brolach steps forward. "I said, give it to me now, slave!"

Jered's body jerks, but Lee keeps hold of him, gathering his hands in hers, to prevent him from fulfilling the command.

"Fine," Brolach says, regaining some composure. "It matters not, not anymore." He nods to his minions, and Lee is pulled from Jered's grasp by invisible hands, joining Rachim, chained in the center of the room.

Jered cries out, reaching for empty air. I focus with Mira's power and my own and place a force field around Jered. But there are only two of us, and there are three of them. The three other Djinn tense, ready for a fight.

"Give it to him," I say. I almost don't recognize my own voice. We cannot come out of this situation on top. Someone is bound to be lost, and I find that intolerable.

Brolach smiles, and I drop the shield. Jered's pained face never leaves Lee's. He doesn't move to comply, but neither does he stop Brolach from reaching around his neck and taking the necklace.

Brolach's own choker immediately falls from his neck, cracked down the center, and he crushes the matching emerald. Then he places the rest over his head. I feel it, the transfer of power, and I press my eyes closed until I see red.

42

DEATH OF A DJINN

"Oh, you are too delicious, Taj! Of course I can't do that. See, I can only kill a Djinni when I've secured another in my service. Safety precautions, you know. That's why they don't die the moment I take them. But if I have all these magicians under my control..." He lets his voice trail off.

"Why would you kill Djinn?" Mira curls her lip in disgust.

"This world is like an infection. It draws the pure Djinn from our rightful home and infects our souls with the filth of humanity. Just look at yourselves! What you've become." He begins to pace.

I guess this is the part where the evil mastermind has to reveal his plan to the superheroes to give us time to come up with a counterplan. The trouble is, I don't see any way out. There are too many of us, and the only ones potentially immune to his power are chained in lead.

"I have to cut out the infection before it can spread and take down our whole species. Rachim had the right idea about closing the door to the worlds, but no one was listening. Everyone wanted the option of popping in and out, like it's that simple. Like it isn't dangerous." He sneers at Achan and Cephas, still bound to their thrones.

"But you're here too," Lee says, sliding onto her stomach, unable to keep her head up any longer.

Brolach approaches her. "Jered, protect me from the lead."

Jered has the same murderous rage in his eyes that I saw when he held a sword to Cephas. But he rises and extends his aura over Brolach's body as he drags Lee up by her shoulders. The lead chains slither off her and into nothingness, and he shakes her lightly.

"I am here because I am the only one strong enough not to be tempted by the sensations of this world." He drags her over to Kitra's throne and pushes her onto it, and her wrists are again bound. "Just a little lead this time, dear. Just enough to keep you still." He steps off the dais and floats to the floor to survey his work.

"Would you like to see how it works?" he asks, his eyes lit with green fire.

I feel Mira's hand tremble slightly, but she betrays no other sign of emotion. I squeeze her in what I can only hope is a reassuring way as Brolach steps forward to look into each Djinni's face.

He stops at Rachim, Jered still trailing behind. The Djinni is barely able to stay on his knees, and Brolach touches his head. "My dear friend. If only you'd picked the other side." Rachim trembles uncontrollably as Brolach pulls a velvet ribbon from the air with a pearl set in its center. He lets it snake around Rachim's wrist, despite the latter's every effort to shake it off.

The lead chains disperse, but Rachim stays put on his knees, eyes wide.

"You'll feel it too," I say. I have to distract Brolach. Anything.

"That's the beauty of it, Taj," he says, turning to me with a dazzling smile. "I don't have to touch him. So it doesn't matter."

He backs away as a leaden knife appears in Rachim's hand. His chest pounds a rhythm I can see right through his shirt.

"Kill yourself," Brolach says over his shoulder, not even bothering to look him in the eye.

Rachim lets out a loud sob that sounds like, "Dira," and thrusts the dagger into his heart.

Searing pain grips my chest, and I fall right along with Rachim. Right along with all of them, including Brolach. All except Lee, who writhes on the throne. Screams sound all around me. But blood pools only on the floor beneath one.

As the invisible hands wring my heart, I throw my head back to look. Sophie tumbles across the marble tile, away from the grip of Caldor, who'd held her up until the last possible moment. Jered is the only one who can react, and he's dropped to his knees beside Rachim, pressing palms over his wound, trying to stop it. But he can't. The moment the lead pierced his heart, it was over.

As soon as Rachim stops twitching, the pain subsides. We scrabble to our feet, and Jered brushes his hand over the vacant green eyes, closing them forever. I think of Qadira and the picture on her nightstand. The tender kiss Rachim gave her when he'd freed her.

And I cry.

Some of the others vomit. I suppose only the three of us have ever actually seen a dead Djinni. I look quickly to Mira. The pain is clear. She is remembering Rhada.

"It is a shame," Brolach says. "I wish no one had to die. But it is the only way to make sure those beyond the veil stay pure. Don't you feel it?" he asks me.

"We all felt it, psycho."

"Not the death. The way your soul feels...*cleaner*?" He draws in a deep breath through his nose like he's scenting the fresh air of a spring meadow.

"You're insane," I say, in case calling him psycho wasn't clear enough.

"You can't feel it," he says, stroking my cheek, "because you've already been compromised by this world. Such a shame." He sounds sad.

"I don't need all of you," he says, staring at me. "So who's next?"

I stare back.

"Taj? Your call."

"Okay then. I say you go next. Set a good example for the rest of us."

He laughs and steps away, scanning the room. My heart stops when his gaze lands on Sophie's motionless body.

43

OCTOBER 31, 1866

"*Let her go?*" *Lucas asks.*

"Just give her the freedom to speak and move about the plantation as she wishes," I say.

"Perhaps you are smitten," Lucas says.

"Hardly. I am not attracted to her in the least."

"Then I can't imagine what does attract you, Taj. But either way, I'm not sure this is such a good idea."

"What did you expect me to ask for? A puppy?"

Lucas stiffens at that, and I wonder if I've gone too far. But he moves to the bed, sitting beside his wife, pulling her into his arms. "I think I can meet you halfway," he says. "Taj, give her back her voice."

"What good is that if I cannot leave this room?" she asks.

Lucas cuts her off with a deep kiss. "Don't be ungrateful," he says, pulling away and squeezing her cheeks in his hands. "And speaking of that little matter Lottie asked you about earlier, Taj..."

"Master?"

"I want a child, and I actually suspect my dear wife here of using magic to prevent it. I'd like you to make sure that isn't the case."

Charlotte stiffens, and her aura grows pink. Lucas is a very observant man.

I move forward, placing a hand on her head. She tries to wriggle away, but I hold her steady, letting my own magic flow over her.

"You should try within the next few days," I say, stepping back. "But you will have to keep an eye on her because she may be able to still use her magic just after copulation to prevent conception."

"I hate you!" she screams, leaping up and beating her fists against my chest.

I stay still and let her get it out.

"I'm glad you didn't sleep with me. I can't think of anything more repulsive," she says when she exhausts herself.

Ouch. That's what I get for trying to help. "Likewise, I'm sure."

"I'm afraid I'm going to have to ask you to stay then," Lucas says. "You will prevent Charlotte from doing anything that might thwart our success."

She falls at my feet again, sobbing, and I bend over to lift her up. She tries to cling to me when I pass her to her husband's arms, and my heart speeds up. In my mind, I see Lee with Achan, and a dull ache creeps through my chest.

Charlotte wanted Lucas. She planned to marry him before he stole me. Now she trembles at the thought of him touching her.

I asked Lee to go to him. I asked her for this.

Suddenly I am ill.

"I don't want him here," she says.

"Nor do I wish to be here."

"But alas, you've already had your wish granted for today," says Lucas.

Charlotte gives me one more pleading look, and for some reason, I decide to try.

"Master Lucas," I say. "There is something I feel it only fair you know before you do this."

"What is it, Taj?" He is wary, but as always, he pauses to listen.

"You should know that I am not attracted to Charlotte."

"So you've said."

"But I am attracted to you."

I let the information sink in. Charlotte looks as though she's about to faint. Lucas clears his throat and stands, tugging his shirt into place.

"I, uh, see," he says. "Thank...thank you for telling me."

44

FORCE OF WILL

No. He means someone else, I tell myself. He isn't interested in killing humans. But I know it isn't true when he slowly crosses the room, stopping to kneel beside her small form. When he reaches out to smooth back her straw-colored hair, I shout out.

"Get away from her!"

He shoots a glance at me, keeping his hand on her forehead. "This child seems to mean something to you, Taj."

"So do all the Djinn in this room. So did you," I say. "Until I realized you were really the sick fuck you are."

"I'm curious," he says, standing. "How it is that Leela there was able to break Kitra's command?"

"Love," I say. I'm speaking loudly, my voice reverberating around the cavernous room because I want to somehow draw him away from her. "Her love for Jered did it. I told you. The love of a Djinni for a human."

"Yes, but I wonder if it might work under other circumstances," he says. "Can you, a Djinni, for example, do the same when being controlled by another Djinni and not a magician?"

My heart races in my chest. I can't do it. I can't possibly be strong enough. I love her. I know that. But it's not the same *kind* of love. Nor do I have half of Leela's strength when it comes down to it. If I'd been through what she's been through, I would have surely broken beyond repair by now.

"So here's what I'm going to do," Brolach continues, drawing out his words. "I'm going to conduct a little experiment. I'm going to command you to kill it. Then I'm going to watch and see whether or not you're able to stop it from happening."

"Please," I say, and I lick my dry lips. "Please. I'll do anything. I'll kill myself. Just let her go. She isn't Djinn. This isn't her battle."

"Bravo," he says. "I do like your verve. But call me sentimental, I don't think I want you to die just yet. I think I'd rather have you watch everyone else go first and then stick around for company while I finish my work."

I look at Lee. Her face is anxious. Jered's hands are pressed to the sides of his head. His eyes cast downward. He can't watch.

"Kill Sophie." Brolach barks the command at me. His eyes are wide, his mouth twisted in an expectant smile. I can almost believe he doesn't know what's going to happen.

I step forward, released from my spot. It seems like an eternity while I cross the room, dropping to my knees at Sophie's side, at Brolach's feet. I hear a whimper. Lee. I reach one shaky hand out, trembling above Sophie's head, and smooth it over her forehead. She is cool to the touch.

In response, she stirs, her eyes fluttering open, sparkling with joy when she sees me above her. But her smile falters when my expression registers in her mind. Then her gaze darts around the room, from person to person, and finally back to me.

A pitiful cry of frustration and rage releases from my throat, and she begins shaking her head back and forth. Her face blurs behind my tears as my hands raise again, of their own accord. I cannot hold it off forever. I must fulfill my command.

"No, Taj. Don't!" It's Jered calling to me. "You don't have to do this."

"I can't," is all I can say. "I can't. I can't."

My hands slide over her shoulders, my fingers creeping up toward her throat. She lies perfectly still as my hands circle her tiny neck. I feel her pulse throb beneath my touch. My tears fall free.

"Taj," she says, and I hold. "Taj, I love you."

"I love you too," I say. But I'm not sure it sounded more than a garbled mess.

"I trust you," she whispers.

I wish with all my being she hadn't. It hurts too damn much. My heart shatters. And my body strains against the command, each muscle on fire. Did I try this hard a thousand years ago when Kitra asked me to hurt Lee? I struggle to remember, just as I've struggled to forget.

I'd accepted it. Hated it. Loathed it. Loathed myself. But I'd already resigned myself to the idea that it was inescapable. I'd withdrawn into my own body, hiding from the reality of it. Each time I pressed the lead to her skin, I cried, I screamed, I swore. But I didn't *try*. Not really.

I am not the same man I was then. We were children. For all intents and purposes, that's what we were. Newborns in our mortal bodies. And we've had a millennium in which to grow in strength and maturity.

They haven't changed. But we have. I know this now about myself. And I know that the one thing I could *never* do is harm Sophie.

With a snarl that sounds like an animal even to me, I wrench my hands away from her neck and throw myself backward on the ground, exhausted from fighting the command.

"Taj!" Sophie is leaning over me now. "You did it!"

"Sophie," I say, still afraid for her to be too near me.

But she smiles at me, and I relax a little. She starts to stand, and Brolach's hand shoots out, knocking her down, where her head smacks the unforgiving marble and she falls silent.

"No!" I scream, but when I reach for him, I'm thrown backward across the room. He still owns me, and I haven't broken that power.

Caldor falls to her side, checking her pulse. He nods, looking relieved. She's alive. But Brolach is headed for me.

"Freeze again, Taj. I'm through with our little experiment for now. And I see the key. I cannot force a Djinni to harm someone they truly love. Fortunately for me, that doesn't have many practical applications." He stops directly above me. "Now that play time's over, who's next?"

"Me." I'm done with his games.

"Very gallant of you," he says. "But I already told you, I don't think so." Then he's spinning his way around the room, hand outstretched, until his finger finally lands.

Pointing at Lee.

45

LEE'S LAST REQUEST

"No!" Jered shouts.

"She is a threat to me. Therefore, she should be next. And if anyone in this world deserves it, it's her. She's the one who started it all, isn't she?" Brolach pokes his finger into Jered's chest. "She wasn't the first to cross, but she was the first to wear one of these." He fingers the diamond on the cord around his neck, and she jerks her head back like she can feel it.

He flicks his hand, and her bonds are released. "Come here and kneel," he says. She complies, stumbling from overexposure to lead. I'm afraid Jered might hyperventilate if he doesn't get it together.

She raises her head, finds Jered's eyes, and speaks. "It's okay, Jered. I want to die."

"What? Leela, you can't mean that."

"I love you. But he's right, at least about me. Look around. This is all because of me. I did this. I am responsible, and I cannot live with that anymore."

"I can't live without you." Jered shakes his head.

"Can I say good-bye?" she asks Brolach.

"You will do it willingly?"

She nods.

"Very well then. You may have a few minutes."

Jered helps her to her feet and pulls her to the side of the room. Of course we can still hear them, but I guess he doesn't care at this point.

"Leela, please don't do this. Please."

"Jered, I'm so sorry. I'm so sorry you had to find that ring."

"I'm not. I couldn't imagine my life without you."

"Don't make this harder. Please, Jered."

"I love you. We'll find a way—"

In my mind, I see her press her fingers to his mouth to stop him. She's probably crying again too. Foolish girl. I'm so angry at her for this I can barely see straight. What gives her the right when we're trying so hard to save her?

I imagine they're kissing again too. Nice, but not the smartest thing to waste time with when you're about to be murdered by a serial killer. I refuse to accept she's doing this herself. That just isn't Lee. She cannot give up like that. After all she's been through. All she's survived.

"Come here," Brolach says. Leela leads Jered over hand in hand.

The knife appears in Lee's hand, and she examines it closely, running a finger along the edge and then sucking at the blood from her finger. Jered pulls her hand from her mouth and kisses the wound tenderly. His aura is a horrible dull gray.

Sophie stirs on the floor in the corner, drawing my eye. No. I don't want her to see this.

Suddenly I'm seized with the picture of her watching as I plunge the knife into my own heart. My pulse races as I turn back to Lee.

Brolach does not give a command, but his eyes tell her he will if she hesitates. So she readies herself, pressing the blade against her wrist.

"No," Jered pleads.

"It will not heal fast enough because of the lead I've been exposed to," she explains gently. "I think I'd rather it this way…"

Brolach nods his assent, and she pulls the knife back with a jerk of her hand. Blood pours from the wound, and I gasp. But she isn't close to death yet, so I haven't really felt it. She switches hands and draws the blade across her other wrist.

The knife clatters to the ground, and Lee sinks to her knees, palms raised, staring at the crimson liquid flowing freely from both sides. Mira is screaming, but I hardly hear it. Jered falls before Lee, cradling her arms in his, letting the blood drench his already soaked clothing.

Lee's breath grows labored; her eyes have trouble focusing on Jered. The other female Djinni lets out a choked sob, and I feel it. The wrenching, like fingers twisting my flesh from the inside out. It overtakes my body, and I fall again to the floor. This time I feel somehow separated from it though, like the pain belongs to someone else. I keep my gaze glued to Lee, who has also fallen, into Jered's lap.

Once again, we are all captive to the pain. But this time, Jered does not try to seal the wounds. Instead, he does the impossible. He grabs for the lead knife, and with shaking hands, he thrusts it through Brolach's heart as the villain writhes on the floor.

Screams of agony assault my ears. I'm almost blinded by the excruciating sensation in my chest, and I know that one of those voices must be mine. But I have no more control over it than any other part of my body. Two Djinn are dying at once, and I'm not sure any of us will survive.

Knowing Lee is one of them, I'm not sure I want to.

46

NOVEMBER 10, 1866

"WHAT IS THE MOST FASCINATING THING YOU'VE EVER DONE?"

I walk with Charlotte through the cotton fields, Lucas finally assenting to letting her free to roam if I keep an eye on her. She is even allowed to give me commands so long as they do not directly bring harm to Lucas, and I repeat them to him at the end of each day. I could shoot myself with a lead bullet for having wasted my request on her. Now I endure more punishment.

"I've battled the Mongols, pillaged with pirates, and shared sleeping quarters with elephants." I know she meant fascinating to her, not me.

"And which was the most enjoyable?" she asks.

"The elephants. By far."

The day is lovely. Cold enough to show our breath, the fields misted with light rain. Neat rows of twisted plants, forced into something orderly. I would be enjoying the sting of the nearly frozen water peppering my skin if it weren't for my charge. If only Caldor walked beside me instead.

"And you've really never been with a woman?"

"I never said that."

"Then you lied?" she asks.

I halt, frustrated. Feel my eyes flash green. She is the last person I care to discuss this with, but apparently she's going to force it. And if I know anything, it is that it is far better to preempt any command through action.

"*Think about it,*" I say, refusing to look at her. "*It's not like I have any real choices of my own, at least not for quite some time now.*"

"*So people have forced you?*" she asks. Her voice is colder than the drops now coming fast from the rapidly graying sky.

"*Yes. To please them. To punish others. It doesn't matter. No one sees me as an actual person. Just a tool to get what they want.*"

"*Yet you gave me over for the same. To Lucas. You threatened me with it the day we met.*"

I do look at her now. Her face is twisted into a grimace, her hands clenched at her sides. Why must we do this now?

"*Charlotte, I regret what I did that day, but I wanted to stop it from happening, and the only way I could think to show you was to let you feel what it's like. But Lucas? I had no choice. Don't you understand that? I must obey the owner of the stone above all else. Above any personal desire or sense of right and wrong. Believe me, if I could have changed things, I would have done so long ago.*"

"*What else have you been forced to do?*" she asks. "*Tell me.*"

"*Everything you can imagine and more. But if you mean on a personal level, I've been asked to torture maim and kill.*"

"*Like my mother.*"

I throw my hands in the air out of pure frustration. "*Your mother understood.*"

"*That you were sent to kill her?*" she screams.

"*Yes. And that I had no more choice than she did. But I was kind. I was gentle.*" I'm fighting my own tears now. I am not the monster that humans seem to think I am. It's all them. "*I've hurt people I loved too! Do you think I wanted to do that?*"

Cal's betrayal. Lee's face. I can't seem to get them out of my mind lately. I tip my fingers to my eyelids and press with all my might, trying to wipe it away.

"*Who?*" she demands.

"*My friend. In the beginning. We had three masters, each owned one of us, but they were all free to give commands, like you are with me. The woman, the one who started this. She hated my friend. Was jealous of her.*" I swallow the lump building in the back of my throat. "*She always gave her the worst of the commands, but she was harsher than just that. She—I believe she received plea-*"

sure from pain inflicted on others. She liked to punish others in any way she could. Human servants, all three of us, but mostly Leela." I sink onto the soft grass, pulling my knees to my chest.

Charlotte kneels beside me, a hand on my arm. But her face is all curiosity. I sigh.

"She pulled us aside one day," I say, and I feel my hands shaking, so I clamp down on my legs to stop it. "She made me..." I cannot say it out loud.

"What did you do?"

"I hurt her," I say, looking Charlotte in the eyes. "I cried and pleaded more than Leela did, but in the end, it was my own hands that hurt her."

It was then that I'd realized the pain Lee had been through. How alone she must have felt those first few months when we shunned her. How hard it was to have put these things on our necks. How she must have struggled.

"Did she hate you for it?" Charlotte asks.

"No." The tears leak through, and I do not stop them. "She never even acted like it was anything. You see, she knew. She understood that it wasn't really me, but Kitra."

"Hmm. And what kind of torture was it?"

I've never had a stronger desire to hurt someone as I do now with this brat.

"Lead. You've seen the effects on me, and most likely on Caldor. She was rather...creative."

Charlotte straightens, offering me a hand. "I'm so glad you opened up to me, Taj. I feel I understand you better now."

47

THE POWER IS MINE

Some of it subsides after a minute, and I'm back to the usually unbearable level of torture, so I turn my head toward Jered. He's rocking Lee's limp form in his arms, his aura flooding over her body, churning waves of gold and silver.

Brolach has stopped moving altogether. The handle of the knife still juts out of his chest. I don't know why, but I find it difficult to look at him like that, despite all he's done. I am immediately ashamed.

I reach for my neck and find it bare. The choker rests, broken, in the middle of the floor where I fell. I realize I owe my freedom—my life—to Jered. It took incredible strength to do what he did while Lee lay dying in his arms.

Sophie joins her brother, nearly slipping in the pool of blood. She must have woken while I was blind with pain. Her face looks fragile, like a piece of porcelain, and I would do anything to take away the hurt. But I'm feeling it too.

Her aura joins Jered's, adding a shimmer of copper to the mix. The pain subsides, and I crawl my way over to them, hand over hand, before I am even strong enough to stand.

I reach for Lee's hand, taking it in my own. Her skin feels cool and soft. *She must be gone, or I wouldn't be able to be here*, I think. I rub my thumb across her wrist, smearing the scarlet stain away. The cut is sealed, a thin white line that fades before my eyes.

But she was right. The lead had given her enough time to bleed out before she healed.

"Help us," Jered whispers like a prayer. But when he places his hand on mine, I realize he's speaking to me. And now I feel what he's doing. What they're doing. They're holding her there, her essence inside her body. Trying to heal her. But she's already bled out. Her heart has stopped beating. Her breath has ceased.

Immediately, I meld my power with theirs, letting Jered guide me. I feel Mira join me and then the others one by one. Wind whips around us until Lee is at the eye of a tornado. I feel her there, dim, but there.

Heal, I will her. *Damn you, Lee, I will* not *let you leave us.*

Then she touches me, seeping into my thoughts like a gentle caress. *Let me go.*

No. You don't get to make that decision. Jered needs you. I need you.

I don't want to remember anymore. Overwhelming sadness. Anger. Fear. Shame.

Neither do I. But I do. That's life. And it's the life I've chosen, so I accept it. But I also remember the good parts. The parts with you, and Sophie. And Jered.

I am opening myself up again. But this time, it feels right. I can let Lee in.

You don't understand.

No. You are the one who does not understand. You're the strong one, Lee. And now you have another chance at love. Remember the promise you made me in the dungeon? If I try, so will you. Well, now it's your turn to try.

You don't know what I've suffered. Not really. Her voice is weak in my mind, quiet and fragile.

Show me then.

Pictures flow over me. Lee's memories filled with torture and grief. Kitra. Cephas. Achan. All of them using her. Using her like a toy in the hands of a careless child. Like a puppet.

Blood. Chains. Hands. Lead.

Pain. Pain. Pain. *Pain.*

So I show her mine. Show her what I've never shared with anyone before. Different from hers, but still the same.

A knife plunged into my neck. Being held in the gazebo and nearly drained. Submerged in a bathtub filled with lead-based paint. The pain of having hurt her.

Silence. It buzzes thick in my ears as I wait, holding my breath, for some sign.

She says no more, fleeing from my mind, but I feel her hand move in mine. Hear her draw a breath.

"She liked to punish others in any way she could. Human servants, all three of us, but mostly Leela." I sink onto the soft grass, pulling my knees to my chest.

Charlotte kneels beside me, a hand on my arm. But her face is all curiosity. I sigh.

"She pulled us aside one day," I say, and I feel my hands shaking, so I clamp down on my legs to stop it. "She made me..." I cannot say it out loud.

"What did you do?"

"I hurt her," I say, looking Charlotte in the eyes. "I cried and pleaded more than Leela did, but in the end, it was my own hands that hurt her."

I wave a hand over my head, and all the blood disappears. I wave again, and both bodies are gone. Though I doubt I will ever stop seeing Brolach's empty face.

Lee's head dips to my shoulder, and I automatically press my cheek to her hair.

"Thank you," she says, grasping my shirt in her fists.

"I couldn't lose you. Not you, Lee."

She brushes her lips against my cheek, and I smile.

I shake myself and realize the three other Djinn are crying on the ground. Mira stands over us, hands pressed against her ears.

"I'm going to take those two home and put them to bed, make sure no one remembers their absence." She nods toward Jered and Sophie.

I nod back, letting her go. Then I rise, making my way over to the others.

I clear my throat. "Thank you all for helping Lee. I'm, um, I'm sorry that I accused you earlier."

The female Djinni stands, wiping at her face. I see she's got piercings in her eyebrows and nose. Her bright-green eyes are surrounded by thick dark makeup. "You freed us. Besides, you were right in a way. We were bound to that asshole."

I laugh at the sound of the word from this girl's lips. It somehow feels so absurd and wonderful at the same time. She seems offended.

"I'm sorry," I say again. "It's just, I think Brolach was wrong." My voice breaks when I say his name. "This world is so amazing. And we are perfect examples of that."

She smiles a lovely smile and sniffles a little. The others have stood as well, and I sense Lee at my back.

"Where will you go now?" I ask them.

"Manhattan," says the girl I've been speaking to. "The village. I want to live like an artist."

"What's your name?" I ask suddenly, not wanting to forget her.

"Talia," she says, and then disappears.

"I'm crossing back over," says the other male Djinni. "I only came for a day, and I've been stuck here as a servant for a hundred years."

I nod, and he leaves without another word. I turn to the last of the three, and without the distraction of trying to save the world, my heart squeezes inside my chest.

He's tall and muscular, just as I remember, and his dark curls are now cropped short and frosted at the tips. Nice. He smiles at me, and my heart does a little flip.

"I told you I'd see you again one day," he says, and the distinct trace of a blush creeps up his almond-colored skin. This time more than my heart responds, and I shift my weight.

"And now that you have, do you plan to take your revenge?" I ask and hold my breath.

He laughs, throwing his head back with relief. "I never meant to take revenge, Taj. I was hurt, angry, frightened, you name it. But I knew you couldn't help whatever happened. All I really wanted was to be able to say good-bye."

"And now?" I prompt, a lump forming in my throat. "Are you crossing back over?"

"We have a lot of catching up to do. And I've had a lot more experience with the world, so I think I'd rather hang around awhile. If that's okay with you."

Yeah. That's okay with me. That's more than okay. "Good. Because I'm going to need your help," I say out loud.

"Anything," he says, a little too quickly.

I raise my eyebrows, and his color deepens even more. But first things first. I turn my attention to Cephas and Achan and wave a hand, releasing them. Lee presses in close to me, and I rest a hand reassuringly on her arm.

"You can't kill us," Achan says, like he isn't too sure about that.

No, unfortunately I can't. I don't have four Djinn.

I take Lee's hand in mine and feel Cal's fingers slip in on my other side. *Concentrate, Taj. Right.* I focus our energy, and Kitra appears seated in her throne, still made of stone. I grin, and Achan cowers at the sight of me.

"Not bad, if I do say so myself," I say, savoring it. She's no longer bound. Instead, Kitra is seated in her usual regal position, arms resting forever at her sides, dressed in the same degrading uniform Lee was wearing. Lee looks down and finds herself in her favorite jeans and tank top.

"You're free. You don't need to do this," Achan is saying.

"Shut up," I tell him, and he snaps his mouth closed, eyes wide. "Sit." He does. Right in his throne. Perfect. "Good-bye."

Cephas's face pales as Achan's turns to marble. He wears my own costume of vest and pants. I savor the moment as the giant searches for an escape.

"I've already been frozen in marble for centuries," he says.

"Too bad she let you out," I say, and then he too is frozen on his throne.

My gaze falls on Kitra's face one last time. I guess I am the leader after all. Who knew?

48

THE MAGICIAN ISSUE

I squeeze both of the hands clasped in mine, but our cheery moment is interrupted by an ominous rumble at the big metal doors to the throne room.

"The magicians," Lee says.

"Oops. Kitra had me televise everything. Guess they figured out they aren't being bound by anything anymore."

"There must be hundreds of them," Cal says.

"If they combine power, Taj." Lee's about to go hysterical. I can hear it.

"They won't," I say. "They never have."

"But they've witnessed it. Some of them."

We all stare at the bulging door for a minute. Then Cal waves his free hand, throwing reinforcements across the back end. Thick metal bars. It won't hold if they combine power. Nothing will.

"We need to go!" Lee says.

"No." I'm surprised to find how firm I sound. "We can't leave this mess. We created it, and we have to fix it."

"How?" Now she's really going hysterical.

"Um." *Yeah. I'm a great leader. Anyone up for a coup?*

"We combine power," Cal offers.

"There's only three of us. It took four to get them all here," Lee says.

Cal seems to have a calming effect on Lee. At least he's drawn her into the conversation.

"We can cross over and bring some Djinn back to help," I suggest.

"You think we can convince anyone to cross over willingly with several hundred magicians waiting to take possession of them on the other side?" Lee barks out a laugh.

"If anyone can, it's Taj."

Wow. Cal squeezes my hand, and my heart melts under his gaze. I've missed him more than I let myself realize. The comfort I feel in his presence is more than anything I've found elsewhere, even in this situation.

"We need Mira. I'll go," Lee says and disappears.

"Let's move somewhere safer," I suggest.

Cal nods and allows me to move us to my upstairs chambers. I didn't know where else to go. But now that I see the king-size canopy bed, I feel the heat flow to my own cheeks.

Luckily, he doesn't seem to notice. He's busy sitting on the corner of the mattress, with his head in his hands, like The Thinker. I admire the curve of his shoulders, the definition of the muscles in his arms. I remember with clarity the way his torso dips into a sculpted V and feel of his well-endowed erection.

I clear my throat. "We'll be fine, you know."

He lifts his head and smiles. "I think so too. I just hate waiting."

"Well, tell me where you've been the last hundred and fifty years or so," I say, sitting so that our thighs touch.

"Pierce was cruel, but he didn't last long. I've been passed around quite a bit. My last master's here somewhere. A woman named Frieda." He frowns and shudders a little. I place an arm around him.

"Was she awful?" I ask.

"She liked to, uh, use me for certain things. And it isn't that she wasn't attractive or even terribly unkind, it's just..." His voice trails off.

"You were thinking of me the whole time?" I ask. Maybe a little too much hope in my voice.

"Exactly," he says, eyes sparkling with both love and mischief. Then when I don't shy away, another adorable grin spreads over his face.

"What about you, Taj?" he asks, his voice like silk. "Are you seeing anyone?"

"I haven't been the best judge of character of late," I say, unable to keep the misery from my voice. I can't believe how well Brolach played me. I should have seen it when Jered attacked him.

Understanding floods Cal's features, and he purses his lips. I've always liked the way they dip in the center on top in a Cupid's bow. I lean in a little, soaking in his scent. Apples and coffee. Mmm.

"If you aren't ready—" he says, caught in my gaze.

I finish the distance between us and kiss him. He tastes like fall. Fall is my favorite season. He moves his mouth against mine, soft at first, then harder and with more abandon. He trails his hands up my arms and hooks them over my shoulders. I pull him closer, splaying my hands across his back. I'm about to throw him on the bed and have my way with him, when Mira clears her throat.

"Again?" she asks.

I pull away and give her a pained look. Does she have to make it sound like I do this all the time? Well, okay, I do. But not for at least a month, and well...

"Again, emergency here, Taj. Or did Lee come to get me as a practical joke?"

"Mir," Lee says, pulling her back a little. "Give him a break. Okay?" She smiles at me.

"Well, now that we're all here," I say, reaching out for their hands. Cal takes my left, Mira my right, and Lee closes the circle.

I focus on the power that blooms at once between our arms, willing it to swell. The breeze blows around us, brushing past my face, tugging at my clothes. I reach out to the others so they can share my thoughts.

Kill them? Mira asks.

I picture Jered and Sophie stuck amid the masses and wonder who else is innocent among them. Many do deserve it, I'm sure.

Immobilize, I say. And I send the power out among those in the castle. I feel most of them swarming the throne room, discovering their frigid masters, no doubt. I will it to happen, and one by one, they too freeze in place.

Memory, I say. I push into their minds, sweeping through room after room until the past month is erased from each one's grasp. Cal starts to ease his hand from mine, but I grasp it tighter.

Disperse. I feel the wind take me as it did the day they came. Plucking each of them from their spot and working my way across the globe, depositing them at random intervals. There's no way I can know who belongs where. But they all have magic, I reason. And we are leaving them alive.

My hands tremble against the others. And I know the magic is slipping away. The energy we've expended today is beyond anything I've ever experienced in this realm. But I force myself forward. Force myself to continue.

Lee falls first. If it was hard on me, I can only imagine what she must have been through. She's one tough Djinni. But as soon as she goes down, Mira and Cal let go, and we all stumble and drop.

"Did we get them all?" Mira breathes.

"A few left," I say. Not sure if it really came out or not. And then all is black.

49

FACING FEELINGS

THE FIRST THING I'M AWARE OF IS THE FEEL OF THE SILK SHEETS AGAINST the bare skin of my back. I fling my eyes open to find Cal's worried face inches from mine. I smile.

"Hey," I say, as he brushes the hair from my face. That feels nice.

"Hey yourself, handsome. How you feeling?"

"Like a tractor just rolled over me and then backed up again," I say, struggling to sit up. I wonder who removed my shirt? And why? But I do enjoy how he bites his lower lip while his gaze drinks me in.

"I'm up here," I say. I love his blush. "Where are the others?"

"They're sweeping the castle for any stragglers," he says, threading his fingers through mine.

"So Lee woke up before me?" I feel a little wounded.

"Well, she was healed by five Djinn and two magicians."

"I guess so." I just don't like appearing weak.

"So about earlier," he says, looking adorably uncomfortable.

"Which part?" I ask, running my fingers down his arm. I watch him shiver.

"The part where Mira said, 'again,'" he admits.

I sigh. "I guess I have a reputation." I don't meet his eyes. "But I don't like it. Not really." *Okay, Taj. Breathe. You're getting good at sharing your feelings. Go with it.*

"I see."

I risk a glance and find him staring at me intently.

"It's hard to open myself up to finding love when I've already had it and lost it," I say. "Also, ever since Lee found Jered, well, I watch what they have, and all I think of is you."

He cups my cheek with his hand, and I lean into him, closing my eyes.

"Well, I don't know if we're going to be Lee-red or anything." I laugh at the name he's given them, and when he continues, I can hear the smile in his voice. "But I'm willing to pick up where we left off if you want."

I open my eyes just as he kisses me. And maybe it's me still a little loopy from all the magic, but I think I feel something in my soul as well as my body.

His touch is gentle yet firm as he slides his hands down my chest, circling my nipple with his thumb. I sigh against him, some of the pressure of the last month seeping out as I cradle his head in my hands, threading my fingers through his luscious hair and clutching him closer. The realization that he's really here, in my arms, in my bed, finally breaks through as tears of relief slip down my face. I've missed him so much. So much that I haven't really let myself get attached to a partner in over a century and a half.

None of them were my Cal.

I flip him over so that I'm on top, and we are both instantly relieved of bothersome clothing. His head falls back on the pillow as I pull away to stare down at his gorgeous face. I reach for his erection, pressed against me, and my own grows uncomfortably hard as I watch his eyes glaze with pleasure. He arches backward.

"I'm not going to last long, Taj," he says through heavy breaths. "I've been dreaming of this moment for a long time."

"Shut up and come for me then," I say, increasing my rhythm and pressure as he squirms beneath me, clutching the sheets in his fists.

"Oh, gods," he cries, cock throbbing in my hand, hot and wet as he erupts with ecstasy.

I roll onto my back and close my eyes, enjoying the moment. He takes me in his mouth, and I thrust my hips at the feel of his expert ministra-tions. His hand dances over the tender flesh between my ass and scrotum, teasing me into an uncontrollable orgasm in the way only an experienced lover can.

Cal flops down next to me as I try to catch my breath, eyes still closed.

"We'll take our time later because I can hardly wait to be inside of you," he says, tracing a heart on my chest with his finger. "We have busi-ness to attend to now, but I'm pretty sure you needed that as much as I did."

We find Mira and Lee in the throne room, decorating the Council statues with various wigs and hats. Even makeup. I shake my head at the sombrero on Cephas's head and the black mustache attached to the stone beneath his nose.

Mira glances over. It's so good to hear her really laugh. It's been ages. I see her take in Cal holding my hand. But she says nothing about it. Lee isn't quite as gracious, however.

"Well, well, well. You better watch it, Taj. He's Djinn. Don't break his heart."

"I don't plan on it." Heat creeps up the back of my neck. "Is everyone gone?" I ask.

"Yup. All gone," Lee says. "And I think it's time we get home, don't you?"

"Yes." I sneak a look at Cal. "See you tonight?"

"See you tonight," he promises, giving me one last kiss that sends shivers down my extremities. Then he disappears.

"I was thinking," Mira says, playing with the corner of a boa she's placed around Kitra's statue.

"A dangerous proposition," I say.

"I was thinking," she says again. "That I might give this world a try. For a little while anyway. If you two don't mind me hanging around?"

Lee doesn't hesitate. She throws her arms around Mira's shoulders in a big hug, squealing. Mira can't hide her smile.

"Only if you promise not to try to chase my man away with your rumors anymore."

"Fine." She disconnects from Lee and gives me an awkward hug. "I knew you'd get us out," she whispers over my shoulder. "You and Lee. You're the strong ones."

I have no words. And that is rare. So Mira kisses my cheek and disappears.

"Home?" Lee asks.

"Home," I agree.

We link hands and materialize in her and Jered's apartment. He's there, waiting on the couch, hands tucked inside his waistband, slouching against the pillows, eyes rolling back to look at the ceiling. But he springs up the second he sees us and runs to fold Lee into his arms.

"Oh, get a room," I say, watching as he nearly inhales her face.

"I was so worried about you," Jered says.

"I didn't want you to see me. I knew you'd do something stupid like come after me," Lee says, plucking at his shirt.

"I will always come after you."

More slurping.

"Ahem."

"Taj, I don't know what to say," Jered says. "I got Leela back because of you."

I rub the back of my neck and try to suppress the grin I feel coming on. "Well, she wasn't going to leave you stuck with me for the next eighty years. No way. It was either this or the aquarium."

"Thank you," he says. And he moves over, opening his arms wide.

"Uh." Oh yes, I am intelligent and expressive. "Yeah." I return his embrace and am surprised to find a warm feeling in my chest. Like with Sophie. Damn, the kid's grown on me, I guess.

"Well, I should probably be going," I say.

"Just a sec," says Jered, steering me toward the hallway. "Can I have a word with you?"

I'll admit I'm curious.

"Taj," he says, leaning into me, eyes all serious. "I'm scared."

"Scared?" I can't keep the disbelief out of my voice. "Of what? You took out the most dangerous being—possibly in this universe—when you shouldn't have been able to."

"That's just it," he says. "I'm not scared of the bogeyman, Taj. I'm scared of myself." He swallows hard and shifts a little. I can see this is serious. "Achan is—was—my father."

"So?"

"So? Genes. I know I shouldn't have been able to kill Brolach, just like you couldn't kill me when I had your stone. But all I knew when I looked at that knife was that he needed to die."

"He did."

"But I didn't hesitate, Taj. There was no 'I'm being forced to do this.' In fact, it was the opposite. It took every ounce of my strength to shove that knife in his heart. But I *wanted* to do it. I wanted him to die. And I..." He swallows again. "I enjoyed it." He whispers the last.

"Jered, I want you to listen to me." I place my hands on either side of him and look him directly in the eyes. "Being here, in this body, means I have emotions like humans do. Like you. Being human means you have feelings, Jered. You love Lee. You know she's been used. Brolach gave you a taste of what that really means, and you snapped. He was a killer. A monster, who was literally murdering the woman you loved and torturing you. No one in their right minds would blame you for feeling the way you did."

He opens his mouth and then shuts it again, nodding. Then, looking off into the distance, he straightens, blowing air from his mouth. As he turns back toward the living room, I grab his arm.

"Hey, kid. You're nothing like him, you know. Nothing."

"Thanks, Taj."

50

DECEMBER 8, 1866

CHARLOTTE IS WITH CHILD. POOR, POOR CHILD. THOUGH IT WILL NO DOUBT end up being just as bad as its mother and father. She's in her rooms now, and I've had a brief respite while she naps. But I know I must head back soon, or she will flog me with complaints until my ears bleed.

As I head toward the double doors to her chambers, I see that one is slightly ajar. I wonder at this only because she normally values her privacy. But when I hear her scream, I'm brought to a sudden halt.

"Oh God, the baby!"

Oh, for pity's sake. I rush forward to close the short distance to the room, and as I burst through the doors, I am aware of something not quite right. The scent of turpentine. The uncomfortable prickling along my arms and neck.

By the time I realize what's happening, it is too late. The bucket perched at the top of the door has fallen, tipping its contents over my head. And I flail like I've been set on fire as she laughs delightedly.

Brilliant red is the shade she's chosen. And it is all I can see. The paint has coated most of my torso, but worst of all is my head. I drop to the rug, rolling in a feeble attempt to wipe the majority away. But in fact, all I succeed in doing is rubbing it further into my skin. I am suddenly grateful for my thick clothing, though from the feel of it, those will burn through shortly.

I am vaguely aware of shouting several very ungentlemanly obscenities at

Charlotte, who uses her magic to tug me along the floor until I hit something cold and hard. I hear the door slam shut.

"Shh," she says, and I quiet.

Then she pulls her invisible ropes, and I am hoisted in the air. The next thing I know, my clothes have vanished, and I am being lowered into a vat of pure pain. My eyes clear just enough for me to realize she's conjured a claw-footed porcelain tub and filled it with paint.

Smoke issues wherever my body touches it. I am writhing so hard, paint splatters up and out of the tub, covering the bed, the walls, the floor, even Charlotte. But there's still more. And still enough to cover my body entirely. The only part of me not submerged is my face.

My body jerks uncontrollably, but I cannot break free of the surface. I'm certain my flesh has been boiled off completely, and I cannot believe I am more than a skeleton ready to disintegrate to dust.

"Oh, poor Taj," Charlotte says, placing her fingertips on my exposed face. "I'm sure that hurts terribly. But I needed you incapacitated so that I could do this." She moves to the bed where I see for the first time, Lucas lies passed out, an empty spirits glass inches from his hand.

She holds up his hand. Where his wedding ring should be sits my stone, mounted in a golden setting. She tugs, but it doesn't come off. "See, he's fixed it so I cannot do this. Because believe me I've tried."

She must be hesitating on purpose because every second is agony. She pulls a butcher knife from the air and whacks his fingers right off. Lucas screams and jolts upright. But she's already cut the ring from his severed digit and stuck it over her own. He sits, clutching his mangled hand, crying. And Charlotte takes her knife and drives it through his back.

I'm going to die. I just don't understand what's taking so long. Surely there is nothing left of me but pain.

Charlotte presses her fingers against my face, and I sink below the surface of the paint. It flows up my nose, into my open mouth, in my eyes. I'm blind. I'm being flayed from the inside out. I cannot breathe.

Then I am yanked out of the paint by the invisible ropes, and I cough and splutter red. I do not know whether it is paint or blood anymore. But as soon as I realize I've seen it, I also realize the paint is gone.

I examine my arms and find ugly blistered skin, torn and bloody. But even *as I watch, it fades to bright pink, and finally my arms are normal again. I am breathing very hard, unable to still my spasming muscles.*

"You may speak again," she says, examining the ring. "I had to quiet you lest you alert someone else or, worse yet, wake him up." She gestures to what's left of her husband on the bed.

I wonder if she's descended from Kitra.

51

LOVE HURTS

Jered pulls Lee into his arms.

I tug a hand through my hair. "Okay then, I guess I'll let you guys get caught up. On things." *Or each other.*

"No. Wait," Lee says. "Jered, we have to talk."

"Lee, this is probably a private moment." I start backing toward the door.

"No, please, Taj, stay."

I shrug and try to make myself scarce by perusing the books on the bookcase.

"What is it?" he asks.

"I have to go."

"Wait, what? Leela, what are you saying?"

I can't help but look, and Jered's face is more contorted than when he was fighting Brolach's commands. Lee sighs heavily and faces me, wringing her hands.

"I'm crossing back over, Jered."

"Leela, you can't! The Grand Canyon…"

"Jered, the time I've had with you was wonderful. The best of my miserable existence. But it isn't fair to you or your family. I've already put you in enough danger."

Jered reaches for her hand, trying to spin her to face him, but she pulls away, crossing her arms in front of her.

"Leela, if this is some stupid attempt to do what's 'best' for me, you can stop right now."

"Jered, we thought it was over, but they came for me. It could happen again. It *will* happen again."

"Then we'll stop them."

"I can't put you through that anymore."

"Did you hear me out there? Is that what this is about?" His voice is an octave too high as he begs her to turn around.

"It doesn't matter why. I just can't. I'm sorry."

"If you're sorry, then don't do this, Leela." Jered grabs her by the shoulders, desperate for her to say it isn't true. I can feel his heart break from here.

Leela scrunches up her face in pain, still turned away from him. But I get a perfect view. Anger wells up inside me again. How can she do this? I wave a hand and freeze Jered in place, agonized expression and all.

"You selfish bitch!" I scream at her. "Do you know what that boy went through? What *I* went through?"

"That's the whole point, Taj."

"I showed you, Lee. You aren't the only one who's suffered. But you are the only one who has an opportunity like this. Look at him."

"Taj—"

"Look at him!" I spin her around, nearly pushing her in his face, and she begins to cry. "I've never known love like yours. Love that can break a command? I would have told you you were crazy if you'd said it a month ago. Nothing can alter the command other than the lack of ability to fulfill it."

She continues to cry, but I force her head up to look in his eyes.

"All you're doing is sentencing him to a life of misery. Yourself to the same."

"But if they come..."

"I will never let them come again, Lee. I swear it."

"You don't have the power," she says.

"Lee, no one does. No one can know the future because it doesn't yet exist. All you can do is live for the time you have." I release my grip, and she falls into my arms crying. I hold on to her tight. "I'm not leaving him. And you shouldn't either."

"I'm scared. I couldn't stand it if he got hurt. Or...or..."

"You don't get to protect him like that, though. It's up to him. You need to let him be his own man."

Leela takes a deep breath and turns back to Jered. She waves a hand, releasing him.

"Leela, please, I love you," he says.

She looks at me, but I remain impassive. It's her call. But I'm sure going to miss her if she goes.

"Maybe," she says, voice small, "maybe we can convince the others to close the door."

"What do you mean?" he asks, grasping on to any possibility as he grasps on to her arms.

"Rachim, before he died, he said if we close the door, those of us on this side will turn mortal. Lose most of our powers."

"Mortal?" he asks.

"I could be human. Be with you like a normal girl."

"I couldn't ask you to give up—"

"I'd do it in a heartbeat if I could. Even without you, Jered. But with you would be much, much better."

She falls into his arms, like it was impossible to stay away, and he holds her to his chest. The next thing I know, they are sucking each other's faces off again. When they get to the little moaning sounds and roaming hands, I slip from the apartment, nearly bumping into Sophie as I close the door behind me.

"Sophie? How did you get here? Did you hear that?"

She shakes her head and takes a sip of her pink milkshake. "I wanted to see you, and next thing I knew, I was here. Aunt Corrie says they're just hormonal."

"I see."

"Want one?" She tips her milkshake toward me in offering as we walk down the hall toward the stairs.

"Sure." I let her conjure one and hand it to me. But when I look, it's brown and not pink. So I frown.

"You wanted chocolate."

"How did you know?" I ask, forever amused by this little magician.

"I heard you. Just like I hear Jered. And Dad."

"But how is that possible? I thought you could only do it with your family."

Sophie shrugs and leads me to the entryway by my hand. "Probably like you said in the castle—it's the power of love. Besides, you are my family, Taj."

I pause outside, soaking in the cold night air. "Sophie? You were right. About letting out the others in the dungeon."

She smiles, clearly thrilled with my admission.

"But I do have a question."

"What's that?"

"You said you followed me to the dungeon. But you couldn't have. Because I disappeared from view. Bent space."

"Oh, I know. I just copied you."

I'm speechless. If any human other than Sophie had that kind of power...I make up my mind immediately that no one else can know, and I tell her so with my thoughts.

"I don't like keeping secrets from Jered and Leela," she says. "But if you're that worried, I won't say anything."

"And I want you to promise me one more thing," I say out loud.

"What's that?"

"Always follow your gut."

52

THE LEADER'S JOB

I TRANSPORT US BACK TO HER HOME AND GLANCE AT THE CLOCK ON THE kitchen counter. One hour until I meet Caldor. I make our empty milkshake glasses disappear and give Sophie a kiss on the head.

"Good night, sweetheart. Get some sleep."

She starts to protest, but I fix her with my best glowing green-eyed glare.

"You're lucky I'm not adjusting your memories," I say.

She makes a little noise like, "humph," and I send her up to bed.

I shake myself and straighten my shirt. I have a job to do. Not a pleasant one either. But I'm the one who has to do it.

I move across space, stepping into the small bungalow in Arcadia, California. It's just as I remember, but not quite as tidy. I find Qadira curled up under an Afghan on the couch, hugging her knees.

"Hello," I say. Good start, I think.

"You? You're alive?" she says, sitting up straight. Her eyes light with hope, and inside, I cringe.

"So it would appear." I step closer, knowing I can't delay the inevitable.

She peers around me, like she's hoping someone else is coming. But I only shake my head. She looks confused for a minute, and then the shadow falls.

"No." Her voice is so small.

"I'm so, so sorry." It sounds terribly wrong. But I don't know what else to say. I'm no good at this. Lee should have come. But she never met Lee. Hell, what am I saying? She saw me for what? Two minutes at the worst moment of her life. Well, until now.

I clear my throat and try again. "Rachim—he was amazing. He saved the world, and I'm not even exaggerating."

She blinks.

"It was my fault," I say then. "I didn't believe him. I thought..." I draw in a deep, fortifying breath and brace myself. "I thought he was the killer. But of course he wasn't, and he was trying to free us. But I had to protect Jered." I know I'm babbling now, but the silence is just too uncomfortable, and I have to get this off my chest.

"What do you mean 'protect Jered'?" she asks quietly.

"He's my sister's boyfriend. A magician. A good magician. I know, right? Anyway, he had our stones, but it was complicated. He did it to help us get away from the others. The Council—they're the ones that started this whole thing a thousand years ago, and he's the son of one of them, but he's good, like I said." I'm not sure I've ever talked this much at one time in my life.

Mercifully, she holds up a hand. I can see she's fighting tears. I stop.

"I know him. Jered. We were trapped in that basement for a while together. We had nothing else to do, so we talked."

"Oh."

"He's a good man."

"Yeah. He is."

She furrows her brow. "Ray was trying to kill him?"

"No. Well, yes. Sort of. Only if he refused to free us, but he still had the bracelet on, and it was really Brolach who was controlling *him*." I'm not doing a very good job at this.

"Brolach is the one who took us? The one who killed Ray?" Her voice breaks ever so slightly at her lover's name.

"Yes."

"He was the last one?"

"Second to last. The last was Brolach. Jered killed him."

Silence.

"As I said before, I am so sorry. But you should know he died as a brave Djinni, and his death was avenged."

"It wasn't your fault, Taj." She examines her hands.

"Well, I didn't kill him, but—"

"I told him to go."

Oh shit, she's crying. Now I really wish Lee were here. "That's what he did, isn't it? You're both part of the Order. That's what it's called, right?"

"Yes," she says, sniffling.

"Well, that's part of who he was, and you couldn't expect to change that."

She smiles through the tears. "Thank you. You know, you're very good at this."

"I am, aren't I?" I ask, sitting next to her on the couch.

She laughs a little and rests her head on my shoulder. "You should join the Order, now that you are free," she says.

"How many Djinn are in it?" I ask.

"Half a dozen. Well, one less now."

"Brolach fooled me," I say, though I'm unsure why I'm sharing this with her. "I thought he might have...cared for me." This whole sharing thing is getting out of hand.

"He was cunning then," Dira says. "To fool you. And powerful."

"And a complete psycho."

She laughs again, and I find myself joining in.

"I think I'd like to meet the others. I'm sure my friends would be interested as well," I say. "It seems to me there is safety in numbers."

"Yes. I think that would be good. We're going to need someone to serve in Rachim's place. I think that could be you. You're good with people."

I am? Huh. I am.

"I have to be going now, Qadira."

"You have a date or something?" she asks.

"Well, as a matter of fact, I do."

"Will you come back? You and your friends? Jered? I'd like the company."

"I think we'd like that too."

53

DECEMBER 10, 1866

CHARLOTTE DECIDES TO TRAVEL. SHE'S TIRED OF BEING "COOPED UP" ON THE plantation. So we head to Europe. To Africa. To South America. It is in Mexico that she meets her end. We are spotted by another magician. A man named Henry Worthby. Worthby traveled from England specifically in hopes of finding a Djinni.

Well, he found me all right. What he didn't realize was that Maria, the young waitress he took to bed to celebrate, was also a magician. Plied with wine and compliments, he told her about me. Bragged about how he could force me to behave.

Three masters in the span of a day. I cannot complain that life is boring.

Maria's such a sweet young thing. We've been traveling for an entire day, and already she's whipped me once. I moved too quickly and frightened her. So she conjured a lead-coated whip as recommended by Worthby and laid right in. For a minute, I thought she meant to murder me, but then she stopped, out of breath, and straightened her dress.

Better than Charlotte, though, I think. Worthby may have explained to her about the lead, but he didn't explain some of the finer points of what I can accomplish. If she understood, she wouldn't be having me buy tickets for trains or ships. She'd name anywhere in the world she wants to go, and there we'd be. But far be it from me to make any unasked-for suggestions.

We're headed back to America. How tiring. I can't seem to escape this infant country. At least it's large. Perhaps we'll try a state I haven't seen yet. Perhaps we'll overthrow the government, and she'll become Maria I, Queen of the States. I chuckle at my own joke.

"What is it?" she asks, eyes flying open.

"Forgive me, I did not mean to wake you." I see no reason to call her Master unless asked.

"That's okay," she says, adjusting her skirts. She isn't used to the overbearing fashions like Charlotte was. But she insists on traveling as a lady.

I smile. She doesn't seem to notice the lack of feeling behind it. Then again, she might not care.

"I still can't believe my luck," she says. "I read the Aladdin and the Magic Lamp story when I was small."

"A child's tale," I say.

"More than three wishes. It's unbelievable."

"The story was based on me," I say.

"Really?"

"Well, no. Not really. But it should have been."

She laughs. I offer her a glass of wine, conjured from the air. She takes it, peering inside suspiciously.

"I cannot harm you," I say. I take the glass from her. As soon as I take a sip, she pulls it back and follows suit. Then she downs it like it's the first thing she's had in a week.

"Thank you," she says.

"You are welcome," I say, refilling her glass.

"Can I have something to eat as well?" she asks.

I try to reel in my surprise and conjure a turkey dinner for her, complete with a silver tray and dressing. She inhales it.

"Oh my God, that's good," she says, leaning back against the seat, patting her stomach.

I clear the dishes and refill her glass. She focuses her own magic and hands me a second glass. I stare at it. I expect this is a trick to see if I know my place. And I also expect to fail miserably as I grab it and gulp. But when she does nothing, I wave a hand, refilling both glasses yet again.

"So what's your name?" she asks, slurring her words a little.

"Taj."

"Mine is Estella."

"Wait. I thought it was Maria?" I say, unable to stop myself.

"I wasn't going to tell that madman my real name," she says. "I can't believe he told me his secret." She fiddles with the stone in her necklace.

"He is an idiot," I agree. "But I cannot tell you how glad I am to be rid of him."

"I'll have to watch out for you, Taj. I can tell you're a real smooth one."

"Oh?" I poke my eyebrows into the sky, and she laughs again.

"I'm sorry I went a tad overboard when beating you earlier. I was afraid you were going to run."

"I cannot escape you now. And apology accepted, so long as it doesn't happen again."

She wiggles a finger, beckoning me closer.

I lean in until my nose nearly touches hers. She smells like spice. Then she whispers, "I can tell you to do anything?"

"Anything within my power. Which is quite a bit."

"You're beautiful."

"Thank you."

"Kiss me."

Oh, here we go again. Curse my vanity, I had to pick such an attractive body. But I finish the distance between us and fulfill my command. I taste salt, and she pushes me away. She wipes at her eyes with the backs of her hands and clears her throat.

"Have I done something to displease you?" I ask.

"No. It isn't you. It's just that I feel nothing when I kiss you."

"Oh."

"I feel nothing when I kiss any man. Though I've learned how to make them think I do. What's wrong with me?"

"Nothing, Estella. I imagine you simply prefer the company of women."

She stares at me, mouth hung ajar. Then she begins to laugh again.

"So I do," she says. "Taj, I'm so glad I didn't kill you."

What a nice thing to say.

Maybe I'll actually manage to have a decade or two of decency. I raise my glass in a toast, and she mirrors the movement. "To new beginnings."

54

NEW BEGINNINGS

"You're here," I say, appearing in my apartment.

"I couldn't wait any longer." Cal stretches out his hands for me, and I take them in my own.

"Well, good. What would you like to do?"

He scrutinizes my apartment, gaze resting for a moment on the aquarium. "What do you usually do on Saturday night as a free Djinni?"

"Find a hot guy and party."

"Well, you have the hot guy, so..."

I kiss him. His lips are as firm and delicious as ever. I let mine linger for a bit, and I drink in the scent of him before pulling back. I find that same warmth spreading through my chest, but it isn't uncomfortable.

"So where's the party?" he asks, voice low.

"What? This isn't enough? I'm hurt."

He laughs, and it is a rich sound that fills my soul. I conjure a bottle of wine and two glasses, offering him a drink. The lights dim, and jazz plays in the background.

"So is your life always this exciting?" he asks, making himself comfortable on the couch.

"Always," I say, sitting beside him and conjuring some finger foods. I feed him some hummus on a pita chip.

"Delicious," he says, wiping at the corner of his mouth.

"Listen," I say, setting down my glass. "We've both just been through a lot."

"Are you already breaking up with me?" he asks.

"No! I just want to get this out in the open."

"Okay. Shoot." He leans back, arms resting across the back of the sofa, and looks intent.

"It's just that I really want this to work. But the truth is I haven't had what I'd call a relationship since, well, since *you*."

His eyebrows nearly disappear into his hair.

"Well, no. I mean, I've done that. A lot. I'm really quite good, better than I used to be, I'd venture to say. But that's not what I'm talking about."

"Taj." Cal leans forward, laying a hand on my knee. Does he know what that does to me? "It's okay. I know we are different people than we used to be. But my feelings for you haven't changed in all this time."

"They haven't?" I can't help but feel a bit relieved.

"I know what you're thinking," he says, and for a moment, I think I somehow put my thoughts on broadcast. "You said it before. You want what Leela and Jered have, but we have to start back at the beginning. Am I right?"

I pick up my glass again and stroke the sides, staring into the dark-purple cab. He waits. I nod.

"You can't just snap your fingers and get back to where we were." He's being literal. Okay. "But what I do know, Taj, is that I loved you then, and the way I felt when I saw you again, when we made love earlier, I'm pretty sure I still love you. I mean, what's not to love? You're hot. You're funny. You're sensitive."

I raise my own eyebrows.

"And you saved not just my life, but like the whole universe."

"Exaggerate much?"

He laughs again, and I smile, enjoying the sound.

"So like you tried to teach me back on the plantation, let's enjoy our time together while we have it and see what happens," he finishes.

"You make it sound so easy," I say, glancing up from my glass.

"It is." He polishes off his wine and pours us both some more.

"Okay, but I have something to say as well." I wait for him to sip his drink and give me his undivided attention. "I love you too, Cal. Those words aren't easy for me to say, but I made the mistake back then of trying to protect your feelings, and that's where I went wrong. I promise to be honest with you from now on." Somewhere around the words *I love you*, I turned my gaze back to my empty wineglass.

"Taj?"

"Hmm?" I ask, conjuring more alcohol and taking a sip.

"Why aren't you looking at me?"

I avoid the question by guzzling until he pries the glass from my hands and releases it to float to the coffee table.

"I really make you that nervous?" he asks, sliding over to put an arm around me.

"Maybe because I actually care what you think." Did I say that out loud?

His chest jiggles with laughter as he presses his mouth to mine. *How about I show you exactly what I think?* he asks inside my mind.

I sink into the kiss because that is all I want or need in this moment. It's like I told Lee: *No one can know the future because it doesn't yet exist. All you can do is live for the time you have.*

And if this isn't living, I don't know what is.

EPILOGUE

MIRA

THE TRUTH IS I'M NOT SURE WHERE TO GO. WHILE I'M EXCITED ABOUT THE possibilities after all these years, I'm also still frightened. Every shadow makes me jump, power ready at my fingertips. Leela has Jered, and now Taj has Cal. So where does that leave me?

I wander the halls of the island palace I've lived in for the better part of the past eight centuries. I knew they wouldn't understand why I remain, so I left with them and then returned to the solitude. It isn't all the bad memories that draw me, of course—it's the few good ones. The handful of time that stands out in my memories like blood against white marble floor.

So many met their end here by my own hands. I couldn't care less about most of them. It wasn't really me, after all, but Kitra, who used me as a weapon. I trail my hand along the rows of souls frozen in marble, remembering each with clarity as I release them, erase their memory, and send them elsewhere. It's what Leela would want, and I've been so vicious to her for so long when my anger should have been placed elsewhere. Leela was easy to hate because I knew she'd continue to love me.

I reach the last row of statues, ending outside the throne room, and pause at the final one. I reach out to stroke his face, something I dared not do when Kitra may have seen. We'd been so careful, Jude and I, yet somehow, she'd gotten wind of our affair. It wouldn't do to let us find any comfort or happiness in Kitra's eyes.

Sorrow weighs my chest down like an anchor in the sea. What could have been...and I hadn't considered that happiness could find me again after Rhada. Now I have a choice to make. Is it fair to release him with his memories intact to suffer a human life at my side? Or is it best to gift him a fresh start of his own, free from the chains of the evil done to him?

I sigh, imagining his soulful eyes coming to life, his full lips soft and warm as they move against mine once again. At first, it was difficult with Jude. I felt like I was betraying Rhada. Then I remembered how she'd encouraged me to experiment with others just as she had. And it had been so long...

Can I do it again? Can I rekindle what we had?

I sigh, allowing my hand to drift down over his outstretched arms, so cold and unyielding. They are nothing like what held and comforted me.

"We both deserve a fresh start," I say. My voice echoes down the empty corridors. I nod, knowing this is best. It's time to stop living in the past.

"Who knows? Maybe fate will have us meet again. If not, you taught me that love can come in the most unexpected places."

I snap my fingers, and he is gone. My gift of freedom feels right. The weight on my heart has lifted, and as I fly up and out through the ceiling, I bid a silent good-bye to the only three statues left inside. They can sink to the bottom of the sea with the rest of Kitra's palace of misery.

Time to start a new adventure.

Thank you for reading! Did you enjoy? Please add your review because nothing helps an author more and encourages readers to take a chance on a book than a review.

Don't miss book three of the *Djinn* series with THE BLISSFUL END available now. Turn the page for a sneak peek!

You can also sign up for the City Owl Press newsletter to receive notice of all book releases!

SNEAK PEEK OF THE BLISSFUL END

PROLOGUE
LEELA

This is the moment I've spent a year longing for. Perhaps it is my nerves making me so dizzy and unsettled. For one who doesn't need sleep, I have been getting my share lately. Jered knows something isn't right, but I haven't let on the full extent of my mystery illness. I do not wish to detract from the big moment or give him or anyone else a reason to postpone for another decade.

Waves of emotion crash over me as I join hands with every Djinn I've come to know over the last millennium. Some far longer than others. Tears flow freely down my face. I could not control it if I tried. Jered, though only a magician, is able to join us as well, because of the sheer number of Djinn present, and I am forever thankful for that as he lends me his strength, enfolding me in his baby-blue aura.

Together we rise in the air, a great circle of beings with glowing eyes in the center of a cyclone of power. We fly upward, slowing time as we go so that it takes a mere flash to reach our destination. Jered has never been in space before. He will be safe with me. With us.

"It feels as though we should have a ceremony or something." Taj speaks through the connection and our minds. He is still new at leading the Order and sounds abashed, which is so unlike him. To me, that lends an air of awe to what we are doing.

"Cal will check the other side one last time," Dira says through the same connection. Her desperation to finish the work her lover started brings a pain to my heart.

Taj nods, squeezing his partner's hand, and Cal disappears through the veil. I hold my breath, but he returns mere moments later with a smile on his face.

"They are ready," Cal reports.

"Let us go through the circle one last time," Taj says, shoulders back. "Say your name and aye if you agree we should close the door permanently."

One by one, starting with Dira, our names are spoken. Every Djinn here is voting yes. It is a mere technicality. I've worked so hard for so long to convince the last stragglers of the importance of it. All I know is that I will finally be free to live a human life with the man I love. My turn can't come fast enough.

"Hold!" Mira appears in the center of our circle. She is holding the hands of Jered's stepsister Sophie and another magician I do not recognize.

Chatter breaks out, but I squeeze Jered's hand, unwilling to let go. Why has she come? Fear grips my heart and causes my palm to sweat. She said she'd stay neutral. She said she'd stay out of it.

"What's with the dramatic entrance?" Taj asks, leaning forward but not breaking the link. Though his words jest, his tone is filled with concern. Both Mira and Sophie mean so much to him. To all of us. But I will not forgive Mira if this is an attempt to stop us. I cannot let that happen. I cannot lose my one chance at happiness.

"You have to listen to me," Mira says in a booming voice that circulates throughout the circle. "You cannot close the veil."

The chatter grows too loud. I grind my teeth together in anger, still holding tight to Jered.

"You have no right!" I scream, and everyone falls silent.

Mira turns to face me, fear in her eyes and something else. Something like emerald fire. When she speaks, it is low and even, a stark contrast to my seething, trembling state. I've been tortured and abused for too long, living in the shadow of fear. I will stop that from happening ever again if it is the last thing I do.

"You did not heed my words once before, and it cost too much. You will hear me this time, Leela. I told you there were too many unknowns."

I know she speaks of her first love, Rhada, but that was centuries ago.

"If this is a way to get even—"

"No. This is to save the one I love and the ones you love, Leela. If you close that veil, then Sophie dies."

CHAPTER 1
MIRA

The velvet blackness of night hides me from view as I creep around the statue of Venus standing guard outside the grand entrance of the Hawaiian mansion. Clever. It's off the grid, but right smack dab in the center of Kahoʻolawe, the supposedly uninhabited island. The perfect place to keep a hidden Djinni and have them create an oasis.

I reach out with my magic and find the magician easily. They're behind the massive house in what feels like a swimming pool. But my real target is on the top level in a large space I assume is the master bedroom.

Despite my cat burglar–like appearance, I go fully invisible and transport inside.

My eyes glow as my blood boils with anger. Bile rises in the back of my throat. There are several women in the room, each one nude and bound by rope at the wrists and ankles. Three are clearly human, and their bodies display recent burns and bruises. Two are not conscious. One shakes, sobbing into the plush carpet with silent tremors. The Djinni, a petite female, smaller than my sister Leela, is bound to the bed by her wrists. Her body twists to the side, as though desperate to hide beneath the covers, and I have no doubt that it is only our aptitude for rapid healing that prevents me from finding any scars on her skin.

I turn her chains to lead and free the other women with a wave of my hand, transporting them to a hospital in Honolulu. Then I appear before the Djinni.

"I am here to free you. I apologize for the lead, but I have to make sure you cannot interfere when I kill your master." I could have said incapacitate, but let's be frank here—he's a dead man swimming.

She nods, tears filling her eyes, and lets out a small whimper. It stings my heart. She will need much attention and care.

"How long?" I ask, voice breaking.

"Twelve years here."

"How many women?"

She looks away. "Twenty-three."

He will suffer twenty-three times over, I decide as I blink out to finish this reign of terror.

The man is tall and lanky, his aura a disgusting mix of putrid yellow and blood red. He relaxes in the jacuzzi, head back against a pillow along the edge. The entire thing is surrounded by candles.

I appear behind him, and the flames of each candle burst high as though they've become tiny blowtorches. I reach down for his hand, resting idly on the deck and rip the large jasper ring from his body along with his finger.

He screams, clutching his hand and twisting to face the threat as I hold my palm open, allowing fire to consume the whole thing. A snap frees the Djinni upstairs so I can concentrate on him.

"What the fuck—"

"No more fucking for you," I state and lift him into the air with magic, turning him to face me. He struggles to move but cannot, and his eyes fill with terror as I reach for his erection.

"Let me, please," a high voice says from behind me.

I turn to find the Djinni from upstairs. She is clothed in a shift dress and holds a dagger in her hand.

I nod, backing away. "When you finish, I have placed an address in his phone." I nod toward the man who cannot even beg for his life. "Qadira will help you get back on your feet."

"I cannot thank you enough."

No doubt exists that this tiny, delicate creature is anything but a fierce survivor. I smile and disappear. I'm supposed to meet some friends.

I clean off the blood on my way to Taj and Cal's apartment. Leela and Jered are there as well when I show up.

"How'd it go?" Leela asks, bouncing over to meet me and pulling me into an awkward embrace.

"Why are there so many sadistic magicians? Is it our blood that makes them sick?" I ask, still disgusted by the assignment I just left.

"Absolute power corrupts absolutely," Taj says, handing me a stiff drink, which I gratefully down and then toss the glass back to him.

"We aren't all perverts," Jered says, pulling Leela into his arms as though being away from her for thirty seconds was just too much.

I know they aren't all bad. I've seen the extremes and everything in between.

"That's not what she said." I nod toward Leela and enjoy both their embarrassment and Taj and Cal's laughter. "So what's the plan? Something tells me that the four of you aren't sitting around playing board games on Friday night."

"We're going clubbing. Tame, I know," Cal says, giving Taj a peck on the cheek. "But dancing seems to be the one thing we can all agree on."

"Well, I won't keep you then. I promised Taj I'd pop by after each collection assignment so he knows I'm okay." I head for the door, but I'm stopped by Leela grasping my hand.

"Please join us tonight, Mir." Her entire demeanor is filled with light and joy. Jered is good for her.

I envy her carefree attitude. She deserves this, though. It is time she had a happily ever after. Taj too. A glance over at him and Caldor, hand in hand, whispering to each other, warms my heart. They've found their loves.

Mine has been dead a thousand years.

"I have work to do," I protest, trying to slip from Leela's grip.

"On Friday night? You can take a break, Mir. You need one. Come on. We're going dancing."

Jered embraces her from behind, and she leans into him. It's so natural, the look on her face pure bliss. It's physically painful to watch, but I'm not sure I'm getting out of it again. I've successfully avoided this for the past month, and I knew my time was running out.

"Fine." I sigh so she'll let go. "But just for a bit."

Leela squeals and claps her hands together in glee. "Let's find you something sexy to wear."

She practically glows, and my chest squeezes so hard I fight not to double over. Instead I force a smile in return and think longingly of the file on my desk at home beside my computer. Dira gave it to me this morning, and the excitement lighting up her eyes had been contagious.

We'd finally gotten a break on the whispers of some of the dark items available on the magician's black market. The market's existence was something the Order hadn't even been aware of until Kitra had us gather all the magicians at her island fortress with the intention of ruling them all. Turns out Cal's previous master had been involved, having procured his stone that way.

I allow Leela to drag me into Taj's master bedroom and snap her fingers, wrapping me into different outfits as I continue to think. The look on her face is touching, though, the way she sizes up whether the clothing does me justice or not before switching to the next outfit. I know she's been secretly pairing up Dira and me since we've both lost our loved ones. Sophie had been at the apartment the other day and mentioned it. It would be a tidy match, no more loose ends and single friends for Leela. But as much as I love Dira as a person, she's more like Lee and Taj—a sibling. The truth is, I can hook up with just about anyone I want, but *wanting* them is the key issue. The roller coaster of emotions and other minutia that go hand in hand with that make me exhausted just thinking about it.

I realize not finding a partner to share my new life with is a problem I've avoided, but when I think back about the two people I've allowed into my life in that way, the heartache at the end is what dwells in my heart instead of the joy of the moments we stole.

That's not how it should be. I know this. But it is a fact, and I do not care to add to this heavy burden because I may not survive another such tragedy.

Leela snaps me into a tight black minidress and heels and at last nods in approval. It's dark and not shiny, which I appreciate. My heart warms knowing she picked it for me and not herself. One look at her nearly neon pink leather and that much is clear.

"Jewelry," she mutters to herself and snaps again.

"How long is this going to take?" I ask, genuinely curious.

She shrugs. "I don't know. I still have to do your hair and makeup."

I nod, resigning myself to the makeover, and the file from my desk appears in my hand. May as well do something while I wait.

Leela makes a small noise of disapproval but continues as though nothing has happened. She won't let me get away with it while out, but she knows me. She knows that throwing myself into the work of the Order has given me a new purpose—a purpose I can handle. One where I'm helping others of our kind while not investing in anymore potential calamities of the heart.

I flip through the file, and something catches my eye. I feel the green sparks pop, making me blink, and am glad that Leela is currently behind me and unable to see the reaction. She may figure out I now have a higher purpose in joining them on the dance floor.

The mysterious mention of DB, or Djinn blood as we've come to suspect, has pinged on one of Dira's searches. Apparently, someone on a 4chan board mentioned a vial of something glowing red being passed to someone at a club in downtown LA called Aladdin. He brought it up in this space in which he foolishly felt secure, commenting that he wanted to try whatever it was. The real black-market boards were harder to access than 4chan, but those were born of actual magic and constantly slid around the Internet through time, space, and dimension. One day we'd be lucky enough to find a magician that would spill the passwords necessary to break it open.

Perhaps today would be the day.

"You know," I say, tossing the folder back through space to my desk across town, "since I'm actually going tonight, how about I pick the club?"

Leela pops in front of me, taking me in from head to toe. "As long as it's an actual club. You know, where we can all have fun."

"Ha-ha. Yes. I heard about this one in LA called Aladdin. My understanding is it's a magician club. I thought maybe it would be fun for Jered and more interesting than a regular one."

Leela narrows her vivid green eyes at me, jutting out a hip. "And this wouldn't have anything to do with a lead?"

I roll my eyes, trying not to react. "Look, if you'd rather I work..."

"Fine. We can try LA. I've never been. But you have to go like this."

A mirror materializes in front of me, and I take in her offer. Yes, the dress is black, but the earrings are about a mile long with crystals that will no doubt catch the lights of the club and make me a showstopper. I don't love attention, but it may work to my advantage tonight. My hair is sleek and loose, spilling over my shoulders and down my back to my waist at its full length because it's been straightened. My face might rival a clown, however, and herein lies the problem.

"One change," I say, snapping to remove the excess and the pink lipstick.

Leela grumbles and snaps again. My new lip color is dark red, like blood, and I look so alluring I almost want to sleep with me.

"Fine," I say, holding out my hand to shake hers. "It's a deal."

Don't stop now. Keep reading with your copy of THE BLISSFUL END.

And find more from Lizzy Gayle at
www.lizzygayle.com

Don't miss book three of the *Djinn* series with THE BLISSFUL END available now, and find more from Lizzy Gayle at www.lizzygayle.com

After a thousand years of suffering, a happily ever after can be hard to accept.

The Order of the Djinn is growing, and Mira throws herself into the work of freeing others of her kind from their dismal fate. It's easier than facing her painful history.

When a magician's black market is discovered to be selling Djinn Blood, Mira's ready to unleash hell on the culprit. But what she finds is far more complicated.

The sexy magician with skills even she can't mimic seems to have a heart of gold and a stubborn streak to match. He not only claims that all the blood has been freely given, but he insists that his purpose is the same as hers. Most disconcerting of all is his uncanny ability to see her in a way no one ever has...even herself.

When those she loves, and the world itself, hang in the balance, will Mira finally trust her heart despite her haunted past?

Please sign up for the City Owl Press newsletter for chances to win special subscriber-only contests and giveaways as well as receiving information on upcoming releases and special excerpts.

All reviews are **welcome** and **appreciated.** Please consider leaving one on your favorite social media and book buying sites.

ACKNOWLEDGMENTS

I promise to make this short and sweet. So many people go in to the making of a book and the support of an author. I have to thank my editor, Tee, for her steadfast support and confidence, as well as Tina and Yelena and everyone at the City Owl team (which is what it really is) for seeing the worth in my Djinn and myself and bringing my dreams to life. Thank you to my forever beta, Leslie, and all who've had input, including Ian and Deborah. Thank you Shona for your constant support.

Thank you to the voices in my head for allowing me to torture you and put you down on paper.

But most of all, thank you to my readers because you're the reason I do this. I cherish each and every comment, review, and interaction I have because the more there is, the more Taj, Leela, and all my characters are given life.

ABOUT THE AUTHOR

LIZZY GAYLE loves paranormal so much, she lives it. She is both an author and a psychic. Between mothering her three kids, attempting to understand her rocket scientist husband, and consistently attempting to declutter her home (that she is convinced is a secret portal to a clutter-creating dimension), she does her best to use her creative  gifts and share them with you. Lizzy is a people person so if you contact her, it will make her very happy and she will likely answer while possibly including pictures of her bunnies and/or bird. She has also been known to write Young Adult under the name Lisa Gail Green.

www.lizzygayle.com

facebook.com/authorlizzygayle
instagram.com/authorlizzygayle

ABOUT THE PUBLISHER

City Owl Press is a cutting edge indie publishing company, bringing the world of romance and speculative fiction to discerning readers.

Escape Your World. Get Lost in Ours!

www.cityowlpress.com

 facebook.com/YourCityOwlPress

twitter.com/cityowlpress

instagram.com/cityowlbooks

pinterest.com/cityowlpress

www.ingramcontent.com/pod-product-compliance
Lightning Source LLC
Chambersburg PA
CBHW031218260626
47169CB00007B/2098

9 781648 981050